What's Wrong with America

Other books by Scott Bradfield in Picador

GREETINGS FROM EARTH
THE HISTORY OF LUMINOUS MOTION

SCOTT BRADFIELD

What's Wrong with America

PICADOR

First published 1994 by Pan Books Ltd

a division of Pan Macmillan Publishers Limited
Cavaye Place London SW10 9PG
and Basingstoke

Associated companies throughout the world

ISBN 0-330-32249-4

1 3 5 7 9 8 6 4 2   06054787

A CIP catalogue record for this book is available from
the British Library

Typeset by CentraCet Limited, Cambridge
Printed by Mackays of Chatham PLC, Kent

'I Thought About You' by Jimmy Van Heusen and Johnny Mercer.
Reprinted by permission of Warner Chappell Music Ltd. and
International Music Publications Ltd.

'You Don't Have To Say You Love Me'. Music by Pino Donaggio
and words by Vito Pallaricini, English words by
Simon Napier-Bell and Vicki Wickham. Copyright © 1965 Edizioni
Musicali Accordo, Italy. Reprinted by permission of
B. Feldman and Co. Ltd., London WC2H 0EA

For E.H.

This book was made possible by a grant from
the National Endowment for the Arts.

October

I

12 October

Dear Kids, Grandkids, In-Laws, Cousins, Assorted Genetic Riff-raff and so on

Well, it's me, your crazy Nana, and guess what? I've decided to keep a journal of my life and experiences, with the reasons for my newfound literary inspirations being twofold. Firstly, just because I've made myself such a stranger to my various progeny and descendants during my lifetime doesn't mean I have to continue this interpersonal omission after I'm dead. And lastly, there could very well be some pretty serious inheritance hassles concerning my estate after I'm gone (more on this later), so I think it wise to keep my kith and kin well-informed about my financial situation.

So, officially, let me begin by saying to wit as follows: I, Emma Delaney O'Hallahan, being of very sound mind and generally sound body, do on this day of 12 October bequeath my experiences to the world in the form of this journal. All my worldly possessions, on the other hand, I bequeath exclusively to you kids and grandkids, but only after I'm dead. And my being dead, incidentally, is the main condition which needs to be fulfilled before anybody is allowed to read this journal.

The house is all paid off and the papers are in my name, so being your grandpa's murderess should not have any deleterious effects on the 'disposition of the inheritance'. More importantly, I have cleaned out our joint savings account and buried it in small bills underneath the rhododendron tree in the back garden, which is only a few feet from where I buried your miserable grandpa.

So now, financially speaking at least, you know just about everything I do.

14 October

Writing is a lot like exercise, in that you should not do too much of it the first few days since you pull all sorts of muscles in your wrist.

Everything is so quiet around here I can't believe it. Last night I slept as sound as a log on the big master bed without being pushed around every few minutes or so by your snorting and smelly old grandpa. I realize it's probably adding insult to injury to say bad things about your grandpa after finishing him off and all, but I have almost forty-five years of concentrated hatred for that awful man still left in my heart, and this will be extremely unhealthy for my spiritual outlook unless I burn it off somehow. So if at times I sound especially nasty, please understand that I'm just trying to work things out in my soul for the bad things I've done, and that I don't mean to send anymore negative karma out into the world, which has enough spiritual poison in it already.

For the second morning in a row I woke after nine o'clock without having to get up and boil Mr Irritable's eggs for breakfast. Cooking Mr Irritable's eggs for breakfast was just like chronic self-abuse, I swear, since he was never happy with a single breakfast I cooked him in forty-five years of servile misery which some people like to call 'marriage'. His eggs were always either too runny or too hard, or the toast too dry or too buttery, and so on and so forth. Meanwhile, I not only had to listen to his complaining all morning but to my own stupid whining as well.

4

'I'm so sorry, dear,' I used to say without really meaning it. 'Would you like me to heat that up for you, honey?' or 'Would you like some fresh juice with that, sweetheart?'

Cooking your grandpa's eggs for breakfast was such an act of self-denial I can hardly believe I did it every single morning for forty-five years!

Having the kitchen to myself this morning was totally strange and wonderful, like vacationing on another planet, or dying and going straight to heaven. For the first morning ever I was able to hear the birds singing in the trees and frogs croaking in the creek behind our back yard fence.

Of course the birds weren't singing in *our* trees, but I hope the radical change of atmosphere around this place will bring them back someday soon. One of your grandpa's seriously unendearing qualities over the years consisted of loading up his twelve-gauge with birdshot every morning and firing it point-blank into the leaves of the high oak and juniper trees in our back yard whenever the birds got too noisy. (This twelve-gauge, of course, being the very same one I loaded up with twenty pellets of #3 buckshot only two mornings ago.)

'Take that, you stupid shit-brains!' your miserable grandpa would tell the birds.

Ha ha. Your stupid grandpa should talk.

From now until my hand gets better at writing long entries I will have a morning entry and an afternoon entry, with time out in between for lunch and a nap. Also: since there are lots of business duties I must perform *muy pronto* to keep the old household finances moving along, I will be too busy to sit around writing all day.

And now, to finish up today's subject, here are some more wholesome advantages I enjoy from not having your miserable grandpa around anymore:

1. Now that his All-Talk radio isn't blasting through the house I can sit down and read my books whenever I want to, which feels so luxurious I can hardly believe it.

5

2. Being able to write in my journal without having to hear your grandpa complain about the bastards of the world who are trying to rob him and destroy this great country of ours, I am actually learning to hear myself think for the first time in my life. For forty-five years the only way I could live in this hell-hole was by learning to *not* hear myself think, if that makes any sense.
3. Listening to the birds and knowing your grandpa won't go firing his twelve-gauge at them ever again.
4. Not having to watch *Wheel of Fortune* every day precisely at seven p.m., even if we're in the middle of a nice meal I've been cooking all day, or a phone call from one of you kids or grandkids (not that any of you call that often – if *ever*!)

Well, I can't seem to think of any other reasons for being happy now that Marvin's permanently defunct in the living department. How funny.

So long until tomorrow.

2

First off it's important to realize that I'm not presenting a very positive role model for you grandkids and I know it. If I was to present a positive role model then I would show a lot more remorse for the terrible things I have done, but I'm afraid I just don't feel any remorse so it would be dishonest of me to pretend I *did* feel any. What a quandary. I think, however, that being honest is a lot more important than being remorseful, so if I'm not teaching you very exemplary marital behavior for a long-standing spouse (i.e. such a spouse should not murder her husband and bury him in the garden, even if he *is* a miserable bastard) then maybe I *am* teaching you a little bit about basic human honesty, as well as being happy with your personal inner nature without trying to repress it all the time.

Being honest with yourself is very difficult, and I should know since I probably didn't commit a single honest act in my entire life. Instead, I just kept my cowardly mouth shut and kept on with the miserable status quo, which probably a much worse role model to provide you grandkids, even compared to first-degree murder.

The other part of my activities which probably isn't a positive role model is that I think I'm going to get away with it – at least for now. Because your grandpa was always firing off his shotgun at the drop of a hat, none of the

7

neigbors seemed to notice when *I* did it. Just this morning, in fact, Mrs Stansfield from next door dropped by as if nothing unusual was going on whatsoever, so I invited her in for a cup of coffee.

'Crime is on the upswing in our community, Emma. And the federal government isn't doing *anything* about it.'

Mrs Stansfield, like everybody else in town, talks to me like I'm a total idiot. She leans forward in her chair and pronounces each word slowly, as if she's working a small rubber ball around in her mouth.

'This means that if us home-loving citizens want to protect ourselves, then it's *our* responsibility. Would *you* like to do something about the terrible crime problem in our community, Emma? Would your husband, *Mister* O'Hallahan, like to do something about it, too?'

Mrs Stansfield has just finished showing me the nice Neighborhood Watch decals and street signs which she is passing out free in the neighborhood. Every few seconds or so I say something stupid like, 'Oh, how nice,' or 'That's sure true, honey,' just so Mrs Stansfield doesn't forget I'm here. Whenever I think Mrs Stansfield expects me to say something interesting, I get terribly nervous and offer to pour her more hot tea. I offer her bagels with cream cheese and crackers with sandwich spreads.

Would she like to stay for dinner? I could maybe pop a roast in the oven.

Mrs Stansfield sighs. I think Mrs Stansfield is even more tired of hearing me offer her sandwiches than I am!

'Maybe some other time, Emma. But what I want to know right now is would you like to join our new Neighborhood Watch program? We'll be having our first community meeting at my house on Tuesday night. *I'll* be providing refreshments.'

I shiver just thinking about it. I take a deep breath and look over my shoulder at the garden. Everything is green and fresh in the garden, especially since I watered just this morning.

'Actually, Mrs Stansfield,' I tell her, 'my husband is upstairs taking a nap, but I think I know what he'd say.

He'd say we don't *need* a Neighborhood Watch program because we already have his excellent gun collection in the den.'

When I took my nap this afternoon a vision of your grandpa came to me in my dream. Remarkably it was not a very scary dream, even though your grandpa was in it.

'Do you think you're being entirely fair?' your grandpa asked me. 'When you tell everybody what a miserable bastard I was, don't you think you're over-exaggerating? I mean, I *did* keep a roof over your head and food on the table. Won't you give me a *little* credit even for that?'

Your grandpa was sitting on the creaky wicker chair which I bought years ago at Cost Plus. He was still wearing the same horrible clothes he wore every day since his retirement. A plaid green-and-red flannel shirt rolled up at the sleeves, faded gray chino slacks and slip-on Hush Puppies without any socks.

I was lying on the bed with the heating pad strapped to my legs. I refused to sit up or take any special notice of your grandpa, mainly on account of my knowing he was just a figment of my hyperactive imagination.

'You were pretty horrible, Marvin,' I tell him. 'I don't mean to be disrespectful of your memory, but I don't miss you one bit.'

'Okay, maybe my temper left a lot to be desired,' he says. 'But I certainly never hit you or the kids – not even once. I have a naturally irascible nature, but that doesn't mean I don't have my loving and compassionate side, too.'

'You always told me I was stupid.' I pretend to close my eyes again, but I keep them open just enough to see him. 'You made fun of my cooking. You called me a brainless moron whenever I messed up recording something on the VCR. You never said anything to me unless it was negative or critical-sounding. It's awfully hard to feel good about yourself if your husband is constantly saying negative things about your intelligence and looks, especially in front of the kids.'

Your grandpa is looking at the bureau, which is cluttered

9

with his smelly old possessions. Hair-spray, Noxzema, vitamins and Valium. Ten years ago Doctor Marsden said Valium might help Marvin relax, but Marvin never took any, since if he relaxed even one iota he might stop driving his entire household totally crazy.

(However, just for an experiment, I personally *did* start taking the Valium on Marvin's prescription, and I've decided it's pretty good.)

He scratches his bald spot. Then he takes his black plastic comb from the bureau and runs it around his thinning forehead, as if he's sifting for gold. 'You do *act* pretty stupid, Emma. It's not because you *are* stupid. You're just a little dippy, that's all.'

This makes me sit up and take notice. I pull the Velcro straps off my legs with a little ripping sound. I am so mad. Mainly I'm just mad that he can still make me mad.

'Well, if you didn't *treat* me like I was stupid all the time, Marvin, I might have more confidence in myself. It's not like *you* were ever such a big genius or anything.'

Marvin is inspecting his black comb. He plucks gray hairs from it and unravels them between his fingers, as if he's opening the pages of some mouldy old book he picked up at a garage sale.

'I just wish you'd stop being so one-sided in your journal,' he says. 'Try to represent me as a three-dimensional human being with complex emotional needs. I may not have been perfect, Emma – but then, who is?'

When I wake up I am sitting just like that, with the heating pad in one hand, looking at the empty wicker chair. Your grandpa's various cosmetic supplies are still lying around the bureau.

Every joint in my body aches. Even my toes are sore.

After a few moments I get up and toss all your grandpa's cosmetic supplies into a big green trash bag and haul them down to the garage.

Then I go back to the master bedroom and take a couple more Valium.

3

16 October

All yesterday after my vision of your grandpa I felt very uneasy, realizing that keeping this journal for posterity is actually a terrible responsibility. Keeping a journal means leaving your mark on history for all posterity to look at and judge whether you knew what you were talking about, or whether you were just another big blabbermouth. This sense of responsibility sometimes makes me a little sick to my stomach, and I even thought of throwing my journal into the garbage can along with your grandpa's hair-spray. Then I thought of breaking my promise to myself and reading back over my journal to fix up its grammar and punctuation (kind of like cleaning your house before company arrives). But finally I didn't and went into the living room for some brandy and a little TV.

(My promise to myself is that I will just tell you every day what I feel and never rewrite or reread *any* of it. This way you can understand my honest feelings as I go along, and it's not like I'm trying to present a picture of myself or tell a story, which is kind of what I've been doing my whole life long. Presenting a picture of myself instead of *being* myself. Does that make any sense?)

All the strange new silence in my house that felt so good two days ago makes me really nervous now. I drink two jiggers of brandy and try to read my book, which is

David Copperfield by Charles Dickens. *David Copperfield* is loosely based on the author's personal experiences working in a blacking factory and living in a debtor's prison when he was little, which is something I know about on account of this very nice introduction to the book by a professor from Harvard University. Though not knowing what either a blacking factory or a debtor's prison are (and not being able to find either of them defined in my *American Heritage Dictionary*), I seem to be enjoying the book anyway. I particularly like David Copperfield's wacky Aunt Betsey Trotwood, who saves David from the deadly Murdstones and hates getting donkeys on her lawn.

Reading books while drinking brandy used to be my sole source of satisfaction when I lived with your horrible grandpa. While he sat with the TV on full blast and complained about the lousy government, I would drink my brandy and drift away into my book, as if I were riding a soft blue boat down a green mossy river. Your grandpa and all he came to represent (men, mainly, and having people tell you what to do, and never being allowed to express yourself, etc.) was drifting farther and farther away, not disappearing altogether but looking relatively unimportant in the General Scheme of Universal Developments. If the book I was reading was really long, I was especially happy, and I traveled especially far. I was in my own world now, a world of clean black words on white, pulpy paper. As long as your stupid grandpa didn't shout at me, or order me around, I could pretend I was in a place where I was totally free and where nobody could tell me what to do, or list for me my numerous personal faults and character problems.

Buying me cheap brandy by the case, incidentally, was one of the few things your grandpa allowed me to spend money on just for myself, since he claimed it helped my PMS, which of course I never really suffered from (unless, of course, he was referring to my pre- *and* post-*Marvin* syndromes!).

My basic worries are this. What if Marvin was not such a bad man after all? What if I really have over-exaggerated all his faults at the expense of his basically good qualities, which I was too selfish and stupid to ever appreciate correctly? He is right, for example, in stating that he never hit me or you kids even once. And maybe most of the times he called me a stupid dog-brain I really deserved it, since I do say pretty silly things sometimes. He never made you kids go work in a blacking factory like poor David Copperfield (a.k.a. Charles Dickens), and we never went to live in a debtor's prison. I guess these are your grandpa's good qualities which should be shown to the world. Just to be fair and three-dimensional, that is.

Finally, I take my brandy up to your grandpa's office, which is filled with books on shelves and stacks of old newspapers and magazines. I have recently made a resolution not to take seriously or subscribe to any books or magazines that your grandpa took seriously, since even if they provided him with truthful information every once in a while they certainly didn't make him very happy as a result – and that goes for me double. These books and/or magazines which never made him (or me) very happy are listed here as follows:

The *New York Times* !!!!!!!!!! (I will indicate the level of disturbance value which these items generated with exclamation points, and the *New York Times* definitely qualifies on my scale of ten as a big fat TEN! Marvin *never* stopped reading or complaining about it!)

The *National Review*, which features your grandpa's hero, William F. Buckley, Jr!! (Two exclamation points.) (Personally I find Mr Buckley only mildly annoying, mainly because I never have any idea what he's talking about, which may be Mr Buckley's only saving grace.)

The *Science of Mental Empowerment Newsletter*, which arrives almost daily in our mailbox, though maybe it only seems that way. The *Science of Mental*

Empowerment Newsletter is the house organ of Colonel Robert Robertson, a former CIA operative who has charted the course of ideal mental activity for human beings over the next century or so. The Colonel's theories can be heard in his own words in a monthly series of taped lectures distributed to his followers for one hundred smackolas a month, to which your grandpa always faithfully subscribed. (And this while he begrudged your poor grandma her paltry thirty dollars per month brandy commission!) In these tapes, the Colonel explains how human minds are prevented from fulfilling their complete potential by a secret group of subversive elements in the universe intent on eliminating free-thinkers everywhere. The Colonel has also written his own personal autobiography, entitled *To Win the Stars*, in which he explains how in his years as a CIA operative he nearly assassinated the Big Three Masters of Destruction: i.e. Joseph Stalin, Mao Tse-Tung, and Fidel Castro, but his plans were always getting mucked up by a lot of liberal spies and pork-barrel congressmen.

Anyway, I give this whole mess of Colonel Robert Robertson's books and newsletters, as well as anything associated with his money-grubbing Church of Reason located in Anaheim, only a ! (one exclamation point) rating. Even though it's probably the nuttiest bill of goods in your grandpa's entire fruit collection, at least it's worth a good laugh every once in a blue moon.

Finally, of course, there are *Time* and *Newsweek*, but since nobody really takes those magazines seriously (especially not your grandpa) I won't rate them at all.

On your grandpa's bulletin board there are all sorts of informative bulletins from the Colonel's Church of Immaculate Reason about local gatherings and lectures which your grandpa sometimes attended. There are also some fragments from your grandpa's book of memoirs, which is stacked on his desk in blue loose-leaf notebooks and which your grandpa has been compiling ever since his retirement. These autobiographical fragments have big fancy-sounding titles, such as *Biggest Lies of the Century* or *Capitalism's Finest Achievements*. Your grandpa said these were 'meditative think-pieces' which readers would come across in the course of his book like, in his words, 'nuggets of gold in a mine shaft'. These think-pieces (or 'nuggets of gold') would make people face the reality of political lies by forcing them to think for themselves, thus sundering their brains from the repressive 'thought manacles' forged by the universe's Masters of Destruction. One of these 'think-pieces' states as follows:

WHAT'S WRONG WITH AMERICA

1. The Russians.
2. The Russians.
3. The Russians.
4. The Russians.
5. The Russians.
6. The Russians.
7. The Russians.
8. The Russians.
9. The Russians.
10. The Coloreds and the Jews.

Well, all I can say is, reading these 'think-pieces' of your grandpa's cheers me up considerably, making me not so filled with self-doubt and worries as I was earlier. Talk about your 'golden nuggets'! These particular 'think-pieces' have made *me* think that your grandpa was obviously a raving lunatic, perhaps even more awful than I ever imagined (if that's possible). So I don't feel so guilty anymore, and fix myself some hot Ovaltine with a little dash of medicinal brandy.

Then I go into the master bedroom and fall fast asleep.

4

In my dream your grandpa says, 'Sure, if you quote it out of context, you can make anything *sound* racist. But I am not, nor have I ever been, a racist person. And in your heart of hearts, Emma, I think you know that.'

Your grandpa's sitting in the wicker chair again. The bedroom is filled with a soft green light, even though all the lamps are turned off and the curtains are drawn.

I have no patience for your grandpa tonight and I tell him so right off: 'You used to call our gardener Mr Ching-Chong, even though his real name was Mr Li. And whenever he came to the back door for his check you'd put your hands together and start bowing and saying, "Vlelly glood, Mlistuh Ching-Chong. Vlelly, vlelly glood!"'

'I was only kidding, Emma.' Your grandpa doesn't have a single trace of self-doubt in his voice. 'And Mr Li always took my jokes in the same spirit in which they were offered. A spirit of mutual camaraderie and good will.'

'You always referred to Russians as crazed members of the evil empire of Slavic Hordes, even when there wasn't any Russia left anymore, just a lot of poor people running around trying to buy vegetables and toilet paper.'

'The Russians are not a nation of free-thinking individuals, Emma, no matter what media slime-lords like Dan Rather try to tell you. They are a negative-capability scenario just waiting to happen. This isn't their fault, but rather the result of titanic universal forces that have been at work for millions of eons. You must understand that I don't hold anything against the Russians *personally*, Emma. All I really care about is universal truth and justice for all mankind.'

'And I suppose your remark about the coloreds and the Jews was also perfectly innocent, Marvin. As if I don't know better.'

'Out of context, Emma – I'm trying to tell you. You neglected to mention to your so-called posterity that my memoirs are not autobiographical, but rather a social satire on contemporary problems of western culture and morality. I would never reduce the coloreds and the Jews to the same sub-category of human existence – in fact, I don't think there's any similarity between them whatsoever. Now, take your coloreds – they go selling drugs and prostitutes in their own neigborhoods, to their own children and babies. But you take your Jews – they only sell drugs and prostitutes in the *colored* neighborhoods. They would never burn down their own homes and businesses like the coloreds do. I can work with Jews, Emma. In fact, as vice-president at Consolidated Mutual, I worked with them often. You might even say that they're my kind of people.'

'Go away, Marvin. I'm trying to sleep.'

'You have to listen to me,' he says. Suddenly there is a strange tone in your grandpa's voice. 'Who else have I got to talk to?'

'I don't care, Marvin. You can't bully me anymore. You can't make me do anything I don't want to.'

'I'm just asking for a little company, Emma. It's cold out there in the garden.'

When I open my eyes, Marvin is looking fondly at my warm bed. He looks a lot dirtier than last time, with bits of dirt and weeds in his hair and clothes. There are dark rings around his eyes, as if he hasn't been sleeping very well. I think I smell something too. Mulch, or strong fertilizer.

This must be because we had the back garden reseeded

about a week before I buried Marvin behind the rose bushes.

When I wake up I feel pretty good, even though your grandpa has tried to disturb me again. Now that I have put my foot down and shown your grandpa what for, maybe he will be less inclined to bother me when I'm sleeping.

I drink my coffee and eat my oat bran. Then I get dressed, put on a little make-up and go open the garage door and warm up the Oldsmobile. It is a sunny day with blue skies and the birds are sitting on our back fence very quietly. They are obviously waiting for your grandpa to come running outside with the shotgun again.

I throw some bread on the lawn and the birds look at me out of the sides of their heads, as if I have a screw loose or something. Then a crazy sparrow jumps down and takes some of the bread, so the jealous robin redbreasts and bluebirds and blackbirds jump down too and start eating the bread and bullying the poor sparrow.

Birds in the yard! I'm so happy.

After warming up the car I drive into town. Mr Sullivan at the bank is very glad to see me as per usual, even though I haven't done up my hair like I usually do before going to see him.

'Top o' the mornin' t'ye, Mrs O'Hallahan,' he tells me in that stupid Irish brogue he always uses on me, even though I'm not the one who's Irish but it's Mr O'Hallahan who's the one. (Actually, my parental families are from Denmark and Wales, though I never saw my family tree or ordered my coat of arms to be certain.) 'And what might I be doin' fer ye this fine mornin', if ye please?'

Mr Sullivan is a man of about my own age who is always smiling and who was once married to a woman named Doris who was almost as miserable and unpleasant as your horrible grandpa. Whenever I saw them together in public Doris was shouting rude things at Mr Sullivan, sitting in her big silver wheelchair like some queenly presence while Mr Sullivan pushed her down aisles at the supermarket, or helped her pick out Easy Reading books at the library.

'You're going too fast!' Doris used to shout, so everybody in the vicinity could hear, or: 'Pick it up, Donald! This isn't a funeral procession!' Then she would hit the sides of her wheelchair with a big wooden cane and everybody within earshot would look at one another and roll their eyes.

What a big B, I, T, C, H, we all used to tell each other with our eyes. Moments like this always made me relatively happy, since most of the time people treated me like I was the Fourth Horseman of the Apocalypse, mainly on account of my being married to your unlikable grandpa. But whenever Mr Sullivan's wife was around, people treated me like I was one of the normal ones – if only so we could gang up together in hating Doris.

But no matter how mean Doris was before her sudden coronary demise, or how crummy the weather, Mr Sullivan has always been in a totally wonderful mood. And now, ever since he started working part-time at the Savings and Loan, he is constantly flirting with me whenever I come in, which is a very positive morale booster for yours truly.

I tell him, 'I would like to deposit Mr O'Hallahan's checks in his account as per usual, Mr Sullivan. Also, he asked me to withdraw money from the same account for this week's household expenses.' I pass Mr Sullivan the pension and social security checks and the stock dividend checks which I have endorsed by forging your grandpa's signature. Then I hand over Mr O'Hallahan's written permission to allow me to withdraw five hundred dollars from his account, which of course I have also forged.

'Looks like Mr O'Hallahan's loosening up the old purse strings,' Mr Sullivan says, and winks at me.

'Mr O'Hallahan wants to do a little more work on the garden,' I tell him. Even though I am lying through my teeth I am suddenly filled with such a flush of joy and well-being that it actually scares me a little. I have to act especially business-like, or else I might start crying with joy and telling Mr Sullivan about how happy I am, and about all the terrible things I've done that don't make me feel one bit guilty.

I take a little breath. Then I unclasp my purse and remove the envelope that came addressed to me personally just yesterday morning.

'And here's another thing,' I tell him, passing Mr Sullivan my social security check, 'I want to open my own savings account. But with nobody else's name on the account but mine.'

First I get your grandpa's Valium prescription renewed at Walgreen's. Then I go shopping for groceries at Sav-Mor, where I buy two large gallon jugs of the best brandy in the house, being Courvoisier which is made in France. Then I load up my shopping cart with every type of canned and frozen food I can lay my hands on. TV dinners, Mrs Paul's fish-sticks, Pringles, beef jerky, pre-cooked barbecued chickens and spare ribs, Sarah Lee pound cakes, boxes of Kraft extra-cheesy Macaroni and Cheese, diet sodas and all the other types of junk food which your grandpa never let me buy since he expected me to cook everything from scratch like his mother used to just so he could complain about it.

Then the nice boy at the check-out stand helps me load the groceries into my Oldsmobile and I drive to the Gardening Shack on Main Street, where this sweet young girl almost as young as one of you grandkids comes to help me.

'I'm looking for some long wooden stakes for the garden,' I tell her. 'To hold up rose bushes and things like that.'

'Here are some sapling poles,' she tells me. 'They are only twenty-five cents apiece.'

I look at the sapling poles. They are about two feet long and very splintery.

'No,' I say finally. 'I need something a lot longer.'

Finally I settle on a half dozen four-foot long aluminum poles with sharp pointy ends and a small wooden mallet. Then I drive home where I take the metal poles and the mallet into the back yard, along with a pitcher of Folger's Instant ice-tea with fresh-cut lemon slices.

Then, without any further ado, I hammer all those metal poles into the place where I buried your lousy grandpa.

'I've had enough of you disturbing my sleep,' I tell him.

I push each stake down until I encounter resistance and give the stake a few really solid blows with the wooden mallet.

After a few solid blows the metal pole hammers in a lot easier, and I hammer it down as far as I can, which is about three feet deep or so. It is still very sunny out and by the time I have hammered all six metal poles into your buried grandpa I have worked up a really healthy sweat, which may not be lady-like but which is very satisfying in a physical sense. It's important to sweat every so often, doctors say, because it takes pressure off your liver and kidneys, especially if you drink a lot of alcohol, which I fully intend doing from now on.

Then I take my empty pitcher back into the kitchen just as the front doorbell rings.

'Hello, Emma,' Mrs Stansfield says. She is craning her head to look over my shoulders, but she's pretending to talk to me. 'Is your husband around? I stopped by earlier to ask about Neighborhood Watch, but he didn't answer the door.'

I feel a hardness developing inside myself. It is an unfamiliar feeling, but at the same time I know it is a hardness that has always been there. I don't want to smile at Mrs Stansfield, or even invite her in for a sandwich.

'Mr O'Hallahan is very tired,' I tell her. 'He was probably asleep upstairs when you rang.'

My voice feels strange. It is as if another person has entered the room and is standing between me and Mrs Stansfield. I can't believe Mrs Stansfield doesn't notice our strange new visitor.

'Oh,' Mrs Stansfield says, 'well, I guess I'll just run along, then,' even though her body doesn't show any intention of running along. She is still leaning in the direction of my back yard. She is still standing on *my* carpet in *my* house.

Mrs Stansfield continues looking over my shoulder at the picture window into our back yard. I turn and look at what she sees. The old rusty shovel leaning against the fence. A wooden mallet on the grass. And six gleaming metal poles sticking up about six inches from the brown dirt near the fence.

'Now, if you don't mind, Mrs Stansfield,' I tell her, 'it's about time I went and fixed my lunch.'

5

Boy, did I drink a lot of brandy!

I wake up way past ten a.m. and don't remember anything whatsoever from last night. However, there is almost one third of the gallon jug of brandy missing. I wonder who drank it?!

Even feeling hungover and getting up late, I still keep pretty close to the schedule I have set myself, which runs a little as follows:

10:00 a.m.   Dance-o-Metrics with Dave and Dana on Channel Forty. I haven't bought proper leotards or anything, but I wear some old pedal-pushers and one of your grandpa's grungy T-shirts and dance all my troubles away each morning to black soul music. When I'm Dance-o-Metricizing, I feel my whole body come alive, even parts of my body I haven't thought about in ages. Some mornings I even start having some pretty wild sexual fantasies above Dave, even though he's happily married to Dana (or so they say).

10:30 a.m.   I take a long hot bath, where I read and listen to classical music on the radio. (P.S. I have finished reading *David Copperfield* and have now started a bestseller I purchased at the supermarket called *Scruples*.)

11:00 a.m. Writing time! This is either my favorite or least favorite part of the day. (I haven't exactly decided yet.) I have converted your grandpa's office into a proper study, which means I have boxed up most of his stupid books and taken them out to the garage, and have removed all his junk from the bulletin board. In place of his stupid 'think-pieces' I have pinned up a few 'think-pieces' of my own, viz:

WHAT'S WRONG WITH AMERICA

1. Too much anger, not enough bread.
2. People with overly critical, negative-sounding vibrations who think they know everything.
3. Shopping malls which are too big and noisy, without anywhere to sit down for a few minutes and rest your feet.
4. Not enough gun control.
5. People who use the word 'coloreds' to refer to people of the negro persuasion.
6. Too many women on Valium, not enough men.
7. People who still blame everything on the poor Russians.
8.
9.
10.

I haven't filled in the last three 'What's Wrong' columns yet, but I'm waiting until I think of some really good ones.

12:00 Noon I fix myself a nice healthy salad for lunch and take a really long nap.

1:30 If it's sunny, I sit out in the garden, or do a little weeding and watering. The roses are blooming wonderfully and the peach trees blossoming. The birds come right up to me on the patio now, where I give them bits of bread to eat.

3:00   This is the time I either go shopping or answer the mail and pay the bills. And every day, as regular as clockwork, I receive more flyers and brochures from Colonel Robert Robertson's Church of Immaculate Reason in Anaheim. These brochures promise to do everything from increasing my self-esteem factors, to debunking my negative vibrations, to contacting my previous carnal entities, to teaching me how to communicate with my pets.

I sure wish they had some suggestions about how to reduce my alarming new influxes of junk mail!

Fat chance.

Today, for example, during correspondence-time I wrote a letter to Colonel Robertson to see what I could do about getting his nutty organization off my back. I began it politely as follows:

Dear Colonel Robertson

Thank you very much for your many concerned cards, letters, magazines, and what-not.

Obviously you people at the Church of Immaculate Reason are very energetic! But please understand that however much I appreciate your energy I am not interested in receiving your highly valuable brochures anymore. Also, it is a big waste of money, since I have no intention of sending you any more checks like my late husband Marvin used to, or subscribing to anymore of your bogus books and magazines.

Ever since my unfortunate husband suffered a fatal accident at the hands of farm machinery, I am now the head of this single-adult household. This means that what I say goes.

Please save both yourself and myself any further trouble by removing my address from your junk-mail lists.

Yours very affectionately,
Emma O'Hallahan

P.S. Best of luck always with your ambitious enterprises.

When I return home from the mailbox I find Mrs Stansfield nosing around the garage door, trying to peek in through the mailbox grate. I suddenly realize that Mrs Stansfield has probably been sitting across the street all day waiting for me to go out so she could resume her snooping.

When I realize this, the hard feeling comes back inside me. I look at Mrs Stansfield and suddenly feel very far away from my own body, standing alone in a haze of pure white light. I am standing in the back yard and holding the shovel I used to bury your grandpa with. I feel very peaceful and secure in a place where nobody like Mrs Stansfield can reach me, not even in a million years.

'Hello, dear,' I tell Mrs Stansfield.

Suddenly I am in my front yard again. I suppose I look 'back to normal', but I don't feel very normal.

Mrs Stansfield suddenly takes her hand out of my mailbox grate and puts it over her heart. She is wearing fuzzy pink slippers, a baggy blue flannel housecoat and reading glasses.

Her face is very pale. She takes a long gasping breath and grabs her chest.

'Don't *do* that to me, Emma,' Mrs Stansfield says. 'You scared the *life* out of me.'

6

MY IDEAS ABOUT ANGER

a personal essay by Emma O'Hallahan

Anger is a concept which develops in your childhood. It is like a big black river of formless darkness. It fills you up on the inside and you spend your entire life trying to keep it hidden. You try to keep it hidden because it is ugly and black. You don't want people to know that this is what your insides look like. But eventually, unless you learn to use your anger, or you secure the services of a really good psychotherapist, this anger gets out, usually when you least expect it. It begins to shape the way your mind thinks. Even little things you do which you think are being nice to people are really expressions of this anger. Like making sandwiches for everybody under the sun, or calling them 'honey'. Because your ideas about being nice and being angry get all mixed up, language becomes a bigger problem than ever before. What you say is never what you mean.

When I watched Mrs Stansfield walking home across the street yesterday I finally started to understand things that have been happening inside me for sixty-nine years. I began to understand that anger is something people control by turning it into language. If you don't know how to turn this anger into language (i.e. telling your husband to cook his own goddamn meals, for instance, or getting a legal divorce from him rather than blowing his brains out with a shotgun) then the anger turns you into something you don't understand. It reaches into every crevice of your body, affecting your tissues, nerve-endings, and blood plasma levels. You can't speak it as words anymore. It has become too big for words.

The anger has become just as big as you are. Maybe even bigger.

Watching Mrs Stansfield, I see she is in a big hurry to cross the street. She keeps looking around very worriedly as if there's tons of traffic or something (actually only one little boy on a Stingray bicycle). She walks across the street. She walks onto her porch. She shakes a lot of keys at her doorknob. She doesn't look back. She keeps shaking the keys at her doorknob and not looking back. Then she opens the door and steps inside.

Finally she turns and looks at me.

I wave.

'Goodnight, honey,' I tell her.

Mrs Stansfield goes into her house and shuts the door. I feel very large and obvious standing in my driveway. One by one, all the lights in Mrs Stansfield's house go on, even though it hasn't gotten dark yet.

I don't know why but the idea of all that wasted electricity fills me with a weird sense of power and sadness, both at the same time.

Poor Mrs Stansfield!

19 October

What a coincidence. Here I am writing my memoirs to you kids and grandkids, and suddenly this very morning I get a letter from one of you! What are the odds of that happening? Probably a million to one.

The letter is from Cassandra, my wild hobo daughter who has not spoken to me in eighteen years. Her letter states to wit as follows:

Dear Mom and Dad

How are you? I'm in New Mexico at the Indian Sisters Healing Center. It has been the most wonderful healing experience of my life so far.

As you must know by now, I have suffered terrible feelings of insecurity and low motivation factors my entire lifetime because of the many poor examples my mother set for me during my formative years. Watching my mother slave away in and be co-opted by the malign patriarchal hegemony made me think I couldn't be happy unless I had a man telling me what to do all the time – no matter how ruthless, cruel, or emotionally unsanitary that man might be.

Through the cultivation of my inner awarenesses with things like Yoga, Zen, psychoanalytical feminism, TM, prana breathing exercises, and learning a trade (in my case, weaving), I have finally reached a point where I can respect and admire myself as a fully functional, caring, and extremely effective individual consciousness. In other words, I am not just another exchangeable bit of dry-goods in the capitalist global economy. I am not some man-magnet, trying to find someone else to make me into what I want to be. I am part of the universal hum and snap. I am independent, sensual, and fully my own woman. When I die, I will return to earth as a cow, a bird, or maybe even an insect.

I can't tell you how much happiness this knowledge gives me.

Only one problem remains, however. Now that I've learned to accept my own inner awarenesses, I really don't have time to keep an eye on Teddy anymore, your precocious grandson who is now almost seventeen years old. And since Teddy's father couldn't care less about him (unless it means figuring new ways to avoid making child-support payments) I would like to send Teddy to stay with you and Dad for a while, or at least until I finish rearranging my inner polarities.

I will send him by bus on Friday, which means he should arrive shortly after you receive this letter.

Love,
Cassie

P.S. All this spiritual growth is teaching me ways not to hate you and Dad anymore. Maybe you guys should give it a try!

P.P.S. Teddy is a very confused young man right now. Good luck with him. I think you'll need it.

After reading Cassie's letter I sit out on the back porch with an early morning glass of brandy (though normally I never touch a drop before five p.m.). At first I think: When it rains, it pours. But then I think: Actually it's probably always been raining and pouring. I just didn't notice it before.

The last time I saw Cassie she was with a fifty-five-year-old shaman named Raoul Stevenson. Cassie was only seventeen at the time and Raoul was already older than Cassie's father (i.e. your miserable grandpa) though of course a lot better looking. Raoul had come by the house to ask your grandpa for five thousand dollars. Cassie and Raoul had figured that for your grandpa to continue supporting Cassie through her eighteenth birthday would cost in the neighborhood of four thousand dollars, and if Cassie decided to go to college, it would cost even more. They promised that Cassie had decided to drop out of high-school and avoid the materialistic concerns of colleges and trade-technical schools to concentrate on becoming a Buddhist, so if we gave her five thou, that would pretty much cover our obligations and they'd never ask for another nickel.

Your grandpa took Raoul upstairs into the office and they came downstairs a half-hour later. Raoul was folding a check into the vest pocket of his Mexican poncho. Cassie was already outside in Raoul's car with her suitcase and some sandwiches I packed for their trip west. She didn't even kiss me goodbye.

Meeting Raoul just for those few short hours had a profound, lasting effect on your crazy grandpa, don't ask me why. Every few years or so he would sit in front of the TV and grow reflective. He would pull at his lower lip and ask for one of my brandies. He would grow somewhat melancholy and self-absorbed, which was probably the closest your grandpa ever got to being bearable.

Then, completely out of the blue, your grandpa would say something like, 'I wonder whatever happened to our daughter's crazy old boyfriend, Raoul?'

7

20 October

All last night I couldn't stop thinking about them. Mrs Stansfield and my grandson, Teddy. Something feels very wrong about the whole situation but I haven't figured out why.

In the middle of last night I woke with a terrible start. I saw shadows on the wicker chair and the moon leaning into the curtains, humming with so much force and gravity I thought it was a broken power line I was hearing. I got out of bed and went to the bedroom door. Everything seemed so strange, like even though everything was totally familiar, this wasn't really my house but only some cleverly designed substitute, like one of those Martian zoos they talk about so much in science-fiction programs.

I could feel the light in the air even before I went to the staircase and looked down. The light was on in the kitchen and the radio was playing All-Talk Radio Night-Line. The announcer, Brent Stickles, was saying:

'Of course everybody always *says* they love their country. But how many of them actually *mean* it? Well, this is Veteran's Night on K-Talk Late-Night, and we're speaking with former Marine Staff-Sargent Boyd Tompkins in Pasadena. Boyd – you're on the air.'

I return to the master bedroom. The moon is bigger and louder than ever. I remove the key from its nail on the bedpost. Then I go to your grandpa's glass-cased gun collection and open the doors. I wonder what I need most – mobility or fire-power? Finally, I choose the Smith and Wesson 4506. I deactivate the thumb-safety switch and go back to the stairs.

'Sure, Brent, I was scared,' Boyd Tompkins is saying on K-Talk. 'So scared I almost pissed my pants. I didn't have any high ideals or anything, you know, about saving democracy or all that. I just wanted to get home alive. I just wanted to see the sun rise one more time.'

When I go downstairs your grandpa is sitting at the table eating a turkey and cheese sandwich on sourdough French bread. He has left the refrigerator door open, which has always been his most annoying habit. He is drinking from a tall glass of non-fat milk.

'It's a hard call,' your grandpa tells me, and removes a bit of lettuce from his lower lip. 'On the one hand, Mrs Stansfield is a very nosy woman. On the other hand, she hasn't exactly got the brains of a rocket scientist or anything. Her husband Ray's just another liberal establishment flunky at the DMV. Between them, I don't think they could figure out the part in Ray's greasy hair.'

I get a sponge from the sink and wipe off the breadboard where your grandpa left bits of meat and mayonnaise. Then I wrap up the sliced turkey breast, replace it in the buzzing fridge and shut the door.

'What if I tell her you went East to visit your family?' I ask him. 'I'll say I put you on the plane. You don't know how long you'll be gone because your sister has cancer.'

Your grandpa shrugs. Then he washes down his last bite of sandwich with the rest of his milk.

After a good long swallow he says, 'I don't think she'll buy it.'

I sit down across from your grandpa. I gesture vaguely with the Smith and Wesson. 'Well, whatever happens, I'll face up to it by myself, and take proper responsibility for everything I've done. I don't need your help, Marvin. I don't need anybody's help but my own.'

'Don't be afraid of anger, Emma,' your grandpa tells me.

33

'Anger is good for you. Anger is Mother Nature's highly ingenious self-protection device. It reminds you of the integrity of who you are and what you won't stand for. It protects you from the savage beasts of the jungle by making you just like them.'

I aim the Smith and Wesson loosely. I put my finger on the trigger. It feels as hard as the thing in my stomach. When I hold the gun on your grandpa I'm not so confused anymore.

'It's time for you to go back to the garden,' I tell him.

Your grandpa looks me directly in the eye and gives me that famous Marvin O'Hallahan smirk. The famous Marvin O'Hallahan smirk tells me that my belief that I am an independent, fully functioning human being is totally ridiculous.

I hate that smirk.

Your grandpa says, 'If I were you, Emma, I wouldn't worry about me. I'd worry about Mrs Stansfield.'

Simple simple simple, I think. Me and your grandpa. Your grandpa and me. Oh yes, and one more thing. This compact and easily affordable Smith and Wesson 4506.

'Go back to the garden, Marvin,' I tell his famous smirk.

And that's when I let him have it.

Right between the eyes.

8

The police are very polite, considerate men who appreciate my sandwiches. I have come to believe that being fully appreciated is one of the most under-rated necessities of modern existence.

'I must have fired all eight rounds,' I tell them. 'My goodness. All I remember is seeing him in the kitchen. Then I guess I just started blasting.'

Officers Lathrop and Rodrigues are sitting with me at the kitchen table drinking coffee and helping themselves to the Sarah Lee pound cake, which is still practically frozen since I never thawed it properly. Through the picture window we can see the entire back yard, where the porch lights are all turned on and everything is lit up like a movie set. We can see the green grass, the gravel pathway, the birdbath, the roses and the bushy rhododendrons. The place where I buried your grandpa and the place where I buried your grandpa's savings are both barely perceptible mounds of different colored dirt. The shovel is still leaning against the fence and the tips of the steel poles are still visible where I hammered them into your disastrous grandpa.

Officer Lathrop is the one with the notebook.

'Let's see if we've got this straight, Mrs O'Hallahan,' he says. 'The suspect was six feet or six-three. Negro, gray slacks, white tennis shoes, and wearing a ski mask. He was carrying your toaster oven when you surprised him in the kitchen. You started firing and the suspect escaped unharmed through the back yard, over the back fence and down towards the creek.'

I pour Officer Rodrigues more coffee and he says thank you very politely. Officer Rodrigues is still picking at the tablecloth for crumbs of the toasted turkey sandwich he just finished eating.

'That's correct, Officer Lathrop. Though I can't remember if he dropped the toaster oven when he started to run, or if I blasted it out of his hands with my Smith and Wesson.'

Officer Lathrop thinks about this a minute. He turns back a page of his notebook and glances at it. Then he looks over his shoulder at the fragments of toaster oven still littering the kitchen floor. Some other things which I hit with the very destructive bullets of the Smith and Wesson in this approximate order are: the window over the sink, the dishes in the drainer, and the wall over the drainer.

After a moment he says, 'I think you may have blasted it, Mrs O'Hallahan.'

By the time I show the good officers back to the front door it's already dawn. The neighbors are still standing around in their concrete driveways, wearing robes and slippers. Children in pajamas are racing each other around trees. The milk truck has arrived, and Dave the milk man is across the street talking to Mrs Stansfield. It's so unusual to see people on the street at all, let alone in their bed clothes, that for a moment I think I must be dreaming. It feels like the entire neighborhood has been turned inside out.

When we come out on the porch, Mrs Stansfield across the street stops talking to Dave the milk man and looks at me. She doesn't wave or smile or anything. Then she says something to Dave and points in my direction.

(Call me old-fashioned, but I was raised to believe that pointing is very rude.)

'Perhaps there are relatives you could stay with,' Officer Rodrigues tells me, a very handsome young Mexican gentleman (though I guess they like to refer to themselves as chicano these days). 'At least until Mr O'Hallahan gets back from his sister's.'

It's so sweet of Officer Rodrigues to worry! It almost makes me forget rude old Mrs Stansfield's pointing.

'No, thank you, Officer Rodrigues,' I tell him. 'But I couldn't stand to be away from my beautiful garden even a single day.'

The officers go back to their impressive black and white car in the driveway. Officer Rodrigues, who is some sort of trainee I think, suddenly looks very reflective and sad, like he can't remember where he left his car keys. He opens the passenger door of the police car. He checks that his gun's in his holster. Then he looks at me and smiles.

Officer Rodrigues has a really big gold tooth in the front of his mouth.

'Thanks very much for the sandwiches,' Officer Rodrigues tells me.

And I tell him, 'You're very welcome, honey.'

9

25 October

What a a busy week! Please excuse me for having neglected my journal the past few days or so.

First off, I had lots of cleaning to do after my foolish activities with your grandpa's Smith and Wesson, not to mention a lot of serious thinking to do as well.

I have had the window replaced in the kitchen, which is so bright and clean it's practically invisible, so Ron the glass-man has Xed it over with adhesive tape. I have plugged up the bullet holes in the wall with grout, and washed down the sink and counter-tops so there isn't any broken glass left lying around. Then, of course, the neighbors have been visiting all the time, with the exception of Mrs Stansfield. And I have had to pay the bills using your grandpa's checkbook, and have met with Jack the insurance man who came over, and hired a neighborhood boy to mow the front lawn, and so on and so forth.

How do writers find time to write every day? It must be very difficult.

I have kept up with my Dance-O-Metrics course on TV, however, so that's at least one good thing.

Still no sign of my grandson Teddy, though.

This week I began digging a new hole in the back yard. It is behind the peach tree, where there's a lot of hard gray dirt near the fence. When neighbors ring my front bell, I lean the shovel against the fence, come inside, and close all the curtains on the yard.

'Hello, Mrs Rheinhardt,' I say to my neighbor at the door. Or: 'Hello, Mrs Francis, or Mrs Snyder, or Mrs Whoever You Are.' Everybody who comes to visit is very sweet and thoughtful. They bring me groceries or chocolates. It is a pleasure to see all of them, with the possible exception of Mrs Stansfield, who is usually nosing around my front yard when she thinks I won't see her. She peeks into the garage through the mailbox grate, or goes around to the fence and stands on a rock and snoops into my back yard.

Mrs Stansfield is becoming a big pain in the You Know What.

I will have more to say about Mrs Stansfield later.

Funny enough, digging a hole in the yard is very invigorating, and fills me with a sense of pride and self-purpose. I am digging a much better hole than I did the last time. I want it to be very deep, with straight sculpted sides and a flat level floor.

I like to dig at night, since I have been having so much company lately I can't seem to get much done during the day.

'You seem very tired-looking,' Mrs Rheinhardt told me yesterday. 'Have you been taking your vitamins? Are you eating properly now that Marvin is away? Or are you neglecting yourself and falling into a rut?' Mrs Rheinhardt brought me home-made soup, which she warmed up in a saucepan. I took a sip and complimented her. Then, after she went home, I poured it down the sink.

Even though everybody tells me I look pale and tired, I think it's probably just because I'm getting older. Actually, I feel very good inside. I have lots of energy and plenty of things to use it on.

At night I turn on the porch lights and the entire yard fills with light. It's almost like being underwater, since I feel very far away from everything. I hear crickets down at the creek, and televisions playing from the neighbors. I'm surprised how calm and peaceful I feel. When I'm digging in the yard I don't think of anything but what I'm doing. I know things will turn out for the best.

According to my personal philosophy, there is a Universal Plan according to which all things occur, and no matter how hard you try to stop them from occurring they will happen anyway, especially if they're ordained by the Plan. There is no sense in trying to work against the flow of the Universal Plan, which is part of the Universal Consciousness — a great thinking Being far more everlasting and perfect than any of us mere mortals. This Thinking Being pays no more attention to us mortals than we do to the cells of our bodies, or the bacteria and proteins in our blood.

But just because the Universal Consciousness doesn't pay attention to us doesn't mean he (or she) doesn't actually love us a lot, too.

I dig into layers of clay and flinty rock with my shovel, and sometimes I take a pick to them. Sometimes when I am tired I just sit down in the damp grass with the shovel in my lap and look up at the sky. The stars seem to be getting closer. I can't explain why. I don't feel so hopelessly alone and solitary anymore. As the Universal Plan progresses, so do I. And in their own way, so do your grandpa and Mrs Stansfield, even though one of them is dead already.

(P.S. *Scruples* has lost my interest, since all anybody cares about in it is money or sex — I can't believe how petty-minded some people can be! Instead of reading, I take long baths with my brandy and a Kit-Kat bar, which makes for a highly potent combination. Better than sex or money any day.)

27 *October*

Finally. I've dreamed about her every night.

Mrs Stansfield has come to visit.

She comes on Friday morning, all dressed up as if she's on official business. She is wearing a nice pant suit and her hair is permed. She is wearing new black shoes with gold buckles on them. I've always wanted shoes with gold buckles on them, but they're what your grandpa used to refer to as 'fancy-schmancy' shoes. Your grandpa always hated anything that was 'fancy-schmancy' – which means, I guess, anything but plaid flannel shirts, gray chinos and brown Hush Puppies. Which being, of course, your grandpa's daily Wardrobe of Gloom.

Mrs Stansfield is carrying her official clipboard and her various Neighborhood Watch pamphlets as if she's going to a convention or something.

'Forgive me for being so nosy, Emma,' she says, 'but I'm putting my foot down right here and now. I want to know what's happening in your house. I know Marvin didn't go to your sister's like you said, since I have been keeping an eye on your garage and your car, and the only time you drove it for two weeks has been when you went to the bank. I have spoken with the milkman and the paperboy, and they haven't seen your husband for about two weeks either. So my conclusion is this. If Marvin left, he left more than two weeks ago, which is about two weeks earlier than you told the policemen yesterday. And if Marvin *didn't* go away two weeks ago then that means he's still hiding in your house, trying to avoid talking to me about my Neighborhood Watch program. Which is it, Emma? You don't need to protect that scoundrel any longer.'

Then Mrs Stansfield rolls her eyes at the ceiling, as if she's about to say a disparaging word about God, or Destiny, or even your miserable grandpa.

'If he's up there,' Mrs Stansfield says, gesturing at the ceiling, 'then tell him to come down here and face me like a man.'

I take a deep breath. I feel a little dizzy. I sit down on my stuffed chair. I'm so happy Mrs Stansfield has come to visit I can't tell you.

Mrs Stansfield goes to the picture window and looks out at the yard.

'It's obvious someone is doing some serious redecorating out there,' Mrs Stansfield says. 'Look, someone's been turning the ground and fertilizing that part near the fence. And look – what's that, Emma?'

Mrs Stansfield leans forward a little more and peers.

'Is someone digging a big hole in your yard?'

Mrs Stansfield steps out onto the patio. I feel a charge in the air, like electricity or insects. Sunny afternoon light is spilling into the house. Mrs Stansfield seems to know what I have to do, and in her own sweet way is trying to help. Even if she doesn't know it yet.

I reach underneath my sofa for the Colt .357, the one Marvin bought himself for his sixty-fifth birthday. I remember that night he sat in the kitchen with a bottle of Jim Beam and took turns aiming his shiny new pistol at the refrigerator, the oven, and the overhead cabinets. Every so often he would start singing to himself and improvising violent sound-effects: 'Happy birthday to me, *pow*. Happy birthday to me, *pow*. Happy birthday, dear Marvin. Happy birthday to me, *pow, pow.*'

Mrs Stansfield is standing on the back porch and looking right at it. It's like the world is moving under my feet, taking me places I've never been before. I feel shaky all over. Mrs Stansfield starts walking towards it. She seems very reverent, as if she's in church or something. I guess she is, in a manner of speaking, just like all of us. The Church of our Heavenly Destiny according to the Universal Plan.

'I'm coming, Mrs Stansfield,' I tell her. Then I get to my feet. My legs are sore all over. I creak as bad as wicker.

I hate getting old.

I am halfway to the picture window when the telephone rings.

Mrs Stansfield is standing over my hole in the yard. Her hands are on her hips. She is leaning forward a little, as if she's balancing herself on the deck of a swaying ship. It's the vast planet-wide ship of the world, I want to tell her. Taking us places whether we want to go there or not.

Mrs Stansfield turns and looks at me over her shoulder.

'This is some hole you've got out here, Emma,' Mrs Stansfield says.

The telephone is still ringing.

I look at the telephone.

Then I look at Mrs Stansfield.

The phone call is from a young lady at Colonel Robert Robertson's Church of Immaculate Reason at Anaheim.

'Hello, Mrs O'Hallahan,' she tells me. 'Is Mr O'Hallahan around, perchance?'

'No,' I tell her. 'I'm afraid Mr O'Hallahan met with a terrible and life-extinguishing accident with farm machinery.'

I am watching Mrs Stansfield kneel down to examine my hole in the garden. I rest the Colt in the folds of my dress. Its weight makes me feel stable, like an anchor on a dinghy. I know so long as I hold tight it won't let me drift away.

'How very unfortunate,' the young lady says. 'My name, by the way, is Deborah St Vincent.'

In the back yard Mrs Stansfield is reaching the tip of one foot into the hole. Very tentative, as if she's testing the surface of a cold swimming pool.

Deborah St Vincent continues. 'I'm a customer rep supervisor with Colonel Robertson's Church of Immaculate Reason, and I was wondering. Would you have time to listen to a brief, inspirational announcement? It won't cost you a penny and it could earn you more happiness than you've ever known.'

'Actually,' I tell her, replacing my hand on the pistol, 'I'm in the middle of something rather important right now.'

'It'll only take a moment,' Deborah St Vincent said.

Then I hear a faint flurry of computerized disco music. Dit-dit-dit-dit-dah-dit-dit-dah. I hear distant, echoing voices, the hiss of electricity, and darkness bristling through buried tunnels. It's as if Deborah St Vincent is calling me from some deep robotic cavern in outer space.

In the back yard, Mrs Stansfield has sat down on the edge of my latest project, dangling her legs and leaning into it.

The telephone says: 'Hello? Is this' – there's a brief staticky rush and a click – 'Mrs Marvin O'Hallahan of 66 Ridgemont Boulevard in Dynamo Valley?'

Another staticky click like punctuation. Colonel Robertson's voice is very cool, handsome and self-contained, as if he's sitting on the beaches of Bermuda with a tall icy drink in his hand, wearing baggy swimming trunks and a floppy straw hat.

'Well, how are you this fine morning?' he asks. 'My name, as you probably well know, is Colonel Robert Robertson, and I'd like to take a few minutes to tell you about my dream. Having recently' – another buzz – 'lost a dear friend or loved one' – hiss – 'you must be feeling very lonely and vulnerable right now. You're beginning to look back over the course of your life and ask yourself a lot of hard, tough questions. Such as, Why am I here? Or, How can I improve my life? Or, What sort of spiritual values do I really care about, and how much money am I willing to spend to feel really good about myself? Are these the sorts of questions that bother *you*? If so, simply answer yes or no into your telephone mouthpiece. Just because this is a recorded announcement doesn't mean I'm not out here *really* listening.'

I stand up. I am holding my Colt in the pouch-pocket of my sun-dress. I feel a little woozy.

I'm almost afraid to look but then I do. Out back, Mrs Stansfield is standing chest-high in my hole in the garden and waving at me.

'Look at me, Emma!' she shouts. 'I'm standing in your hole in the yard!'

I know, I want to tell her. It's obvious.

'I really have to be going, Colonel Robertson,' I tell him. (I can't believe it, but I feel I should be polite even to a

44

recording!) 'And I'm afraid that, since I'm not another sucker like my recently extinct husband, I won't be sending you anymore of our hard-earned savings, either. So please don't bother calling here anymore.'

'Well, of *course* you do,' the Colonel's pre-recorded voice tells me. 'They're the sorts of questions *everyone* asks themselves – it's only *natural*. That's why we here at the Church have devised a new video-taped instruction manual for our members, new and old. If you'd like to send us $29.99, then in return we'll send you—'

I hang up on the Colonel and feel a long subsiding hiss in the room around me, as if someone's spraying a can of aerosol home deodorant. I go to the picture window. Mrs Stansfield is kneeling in the bottom of the hole so only the top of her head is visible.

She looks up.

'You could bury an *army* in here, Emma,' Mrs Stansfield says. 'And look what I found.'

She stands and shows me something in her hand. It's clayey and thin.

I can't see this far without my glasses.

'An Indian arrowhead,' Mrs Stansfield tells me. 'Come here, Emma. Let me show you.'

'I'm coming,' I say. I let myself down slowly from the picture window and onto the wooden patio. I'm carefully holding the gun in my pocket so it doesn't accidentally get knocked against anything.

The Universal Plan tells us all what to do. And when we know there's a reason for everything, we don't feel so scared or alone. That's sort of what Colonel Robertson wants to tell me, but only if I hand over loads of cash.

'I'll be right there, Mrs Stansfield,' I tell her. 'Hold onto your horses. I'll be there in a minute.'

November

IO

Well, keeping up with my daily journal entries has become very trying lately, so instead of punishing myself all the time for skipping days or not making my entries long enough, I will now adopt a looser, more undated writing format. When I have time to recount my daily adventures, I will do so. And when I don't have time, I won't recount them. In the meantime I will try to be kind to myself whenever I don't get a lot of work done, or come up with any sensible philosophical or political ideas to pass on to my progeny. After sixty-nine years of existence it's about time I started giving myself a little credit. Just because I have 'broken out' of the cocoon of my life with Marvin doesn't mean I'm going to be an overnight sensation in the profession of journal writing! An achievement like that, of course, would take many months of dedicated effort.

'Go easy on yourself, Emma.' That's my new motto.

I guess my daily schedule has gotten pretty screwed up lately. I've been waking up later and later in the morning, even in the afternoons sometimes. I've been intending to fix myself salads for lunch and then do my writing in the study, but sometimes I start watching one of my favorite afternoon soap operas on TV, like *Loving to Share* or *Strangers Forever*. Then maybe I'll have a glass of brandy and a Kit-Kat bar, and before I know it I'm watching *Jeopardy* on TV (which means it's seven-thirty p.m. already), or taking another long nap. I have needed lots of naps lately to cope with the pressures of my current existence. Or maybe I'm still coping with the pressures of my former existence with Marvin.

Or maybe I'm just getting old. Who knows?

For days I get like this, going from one nap to another, drinking my brandy at weird hours of the day and night, eating too many Kit-Kat bars and frozen food. Many nights I find myself sitting up watching Cal Worthington and his dog Spot. Cal hosts the all-night movie program, which is really just this elaborate excuse to show jillions of car commercials. I sit around eating Pringles, drinking brandy, and wondering what I did all day long to get here. I can't remember what time I woke, or what TV programs I watched, or whether anybody came to visit, or even whether I went shopping or not.

These problems are partly because I haven't been keeping my journal, and partly because I keep *forgetting* to keep my journal. Which are two separate problems, I think.

I do remember a few highly important events (or non-events), however, such as the following:

1. My grandson Teddy has not arrived yet, and I haven't called his mother in Santa Fe because I don't want to worry her.
2. I have continued receiving many good-sized checks from your grandpa's various investments and my own monthly social security checks, all of which I've been meaning to take to the bank.
3. I have been walking up to the corner Stop-and-Shop a lot lately, which is why I still have plenty of unexpired junk-food in the kitchen cabinets.
4. I don't remember driving to the bank even once in the past few weeks, but I still have plenty of cash in my wallet. What is more, I haven't dug up your grandpa's savings from the garden even once. (No sense being extravagant.)

One day recently, though, I did receive a call from Thomas, my son, which means it must have been close to the first of the month already, since that's when we usually get our social security checks.

'Hello, Mom,' Thomas says as per usual. 'Dad around?'

'Dad's in Connecticut,' I tell him. 'He went to visit his sister who has cancer.'

'Really?' Thomas says. 'Far out.' Then I hear Thomas call over his shoulder to his wife Mary-Lou. 'Hey, babe! My old man went on a *trip*. Yeah – like *out of town*, man. He actually left the *house*. Can you dig it?'

I hate when Thomas says, 'dig it'. I don't know why exactly. I just do.

Then Thomas says to me: 'I didn't even know Dad *had* a sister.'

'Well,' I tell him, 'he does. And now she's got cancer.'

'Oh,' Thomas says, as if he has to think about this for a minute. Then, kind of like a distraction, he says, 'So how are you, Mom?' This is what he usually says whenever he's killing time waiting for his father to come to the phone.

Thomas is the fruit of my womb but otherwise we are not related whatsoever.

'I have been getting a lot of rest, sweetheart,' I tell him. 'How are Mary-Lou and the grandkids?'

'They're fine, Mom. Oh, and yeah. Thanks for the checks. We deposited them in the kids' college accounts, just like you asked.'

I sent them checks? Boy, I really *am* getting pretty sloppy, memory-wise.

'That's very good, sweetheart. Now, Thomas, I want to try telling you something, and I don't want you to get upset or anything.'

'Oh, yeah?' Thomas's voice goes very soft suddenly. I can't tell whether it's because I've captured his attention for once, or whether he's trying to follow some ball game on TV. I can hear Al Michaels saying in the background: 'Talk about blocking for offense – he literally took that guy's head off!'

I tell my son Thomas the following: 'I just want you to know, Thomas, that I have divided the estate equally between you and your sister, Cassie, in Santa Fe, and that it will be coming directly to you now upon our demise, and not be left to Colonel Robertson's Church of Immaculate Reason like your father originally intended. I have not had all the paperwork done yet, but when I do get it done I'll have a copy sent to you through your father's lawyer, Mr Oswald Spengler.'

I hear Thomas take a long deep breath.

'Wow, Mom. Like how in the world did you ever arrange *that*?'

I try to ignore his question and just carry on with my confession before I lose my nerve.

'Also, Thomas, I would like you to know that, whatever happens, your father really did love you in his own special way. I know it was such a special way that it was pretty hard to notice most of the time, but he really did. And I'm sorry you had so many fights with him about money, and I wish I had helped out more. But I had to live with him and you didn't. I guess that's how I looked at it. I was very selfish then and now I'm sorry.'

Thomas doesn't say anything for a while. In the background I hear his wife Mary-Lou doing dishes in the sink, cutlery clattering.

After a while I say, 'Thomas?'

'Yeah, Mom.'

'Did you hear what I said?'

And my thirty-eight-year-old son tells me: 'I heard, Mom. It's just a whole lot of truth to deal with in one batch. Know what I mean?'

I sure do.

So I tell him: 'I know it's unusual, sweetheart. Truth is a very tricky idea to get used to.'

I cried for an hour in the guest bathroom with the door locked, even though I could've used the living room if I'd wanted. Old habits die hard, I guess. I went through a whole roll of toilet paper.

Then I took a long bath and twice refused myself a glass of brandy. My face looked all red and runny in the mirror.

It's time you shape up, Emma, I told myself. You're going to hell in a handbasket.

I went to bed early with my new book, which is *The Great Short Stories of Anton Chekhov*, a Russian writer whose stories are very sadly composed. But instead of reading the Chekhov stories I rested the book on my knee, which is a position which often helps me think about things truthfully and honestly. Then I tried giving myself a pep talk, of which I am in sore need these days.

My pep talk to myself goes a little something like this:

Well, Emma, obviously you have pulled a few boners recently. I don't mean Marvin, who had it coming to him, but poor Mrs Stansfield, who was not a bad or evil woman, and really didn't deserve what happened to her whatsoever. And you don't even know what happened to her exactly, except that now she is buried in the garden along with Marvin and your savings account, and this is not the best way to solve interpersonal problems, that's for darn sure. Yes, Mrs Stansfield was nosy. Yes, she treated you condescendingly, and never respected your opinion about anything, and treated you like Marvin's pet drone. But on the other hand she was right to believe that your opinions weren't worth much, and in your own flaky way you are pretty dronish, actually.

Okay, so you've made your share of mistakes. But now that you're on your own in life, you'll have to accept yourself both for good and bad. You can't blame all your mistakes on Marvin like you used to, since you're not his slave anymore, and being free of slavery means taking responsibilities for all your own actions. Making decisions on your own will be hard work, and you have to be kind to yourself when you make a wrong one. So what I want you to do right this minute, Emma, is take out a piece of paper in your journal and write down a list of qualities you admire about yourself. And I want you to do it *right this minute*!

LIST OF QUALITIES I ADMIRE MOST
ABOUT MYSELF

by Emma O'Hallahan

1. I have learned to take responsibility for my own actions, and do not blame them all on my horrible life, or on the way I was treated by Marvin, which is what the younger generation refers to as 'a royal cop-out'.
2. I am dealing with a very difficult series of personal situations the best I can, and there's nothing more a person can ever ask from him or herself except the best they can.
3. I finally realize my drinking and body-management problems are getting the best of me, and I will do everything I can to correct them *muy pronto*.
4. Neither Marvin nor Mrs Stansfield suffered unnecessarily (at least not that I can remember!).
5. I will greet my grandson Teddy with open arms and generous offerings of my home and savings. If and when he arrives, that is.
6. I am essentially a good person with good intentions. It's just that sometimes I make mistakes of judgment, mainly because judgment is not something I've had much experience doing on my own before.
7. I see through crazy charlatans like Colonel Robertson or my ex-husband Marvin, even though they pretend *they're* the ones who are such big geniuses all the time.
8. I am doing everything I can to improve myself and my life. And I am doing my very best to make up for whatever mistakes I may commit along the way.

So there you are, Emma O'Hallahan – all your best qualities listed for posterity to read about and admire. In other words, you haven't got anything to be embarrassed about, old girl. Maybe nobody else is – but *I'm* proud of you!

I I

28 October

Oswald T. Spengler,
Harbinson, Wallecki, Jones and Spengler,
Studio City CA 90024

Dear Mrs O'Hallahan

Pursuant and forthwith regarding the termination of your husband's fiduciary interests viz. henceforth and legally pertaining to. The executorial strictures required by Item #77 in the California Jurisprudence Code of 1983 regarding land-grant management habba habba and thus responsible forthwith to and fro as follows blah blah blah, blah blah blahblahblah. The disposition of all properties must be co-signed and co-dependent upon birth registration and legal parental etcetera, etcetera, yours very kindly, your husband's hot-shot big-mouth obnoxious lawyer with the greasy hair and the alligator shoes,

Oswald T. Spengler

P.S.   I would advise immediate personal counseling as regards your husband's frequent rejoinders occurring per example in letters to this office and other concerned parties dated 4-15-81, 3-6-83, 7-30-83, etcetera etcetera. How about Thursday?

Note to progeny: As you may notice, I haven't actually included the original copy of this delightful letter which I recently received from your miserable grandpa's lawer. Instead I have tried to jot down my general recollection thereof, since this aforesaid letter got me so riled up that I tore it into a jillion trillion pieces and fed them down the garbage disposal – which is, quite frankly, exactly what I'd *like* to do to Mr Brainiac Lawyer.

If Mr Spengler was even remotely human, his letter to me might have gone a little bit as follows:

> Dear Emma
>
> I'm afraid I can't change your miserable bastard of a husband's will quite so easily as you suppose! First I'll need him to sign a few documents for me, which I could bring over later this week. How's that sound?
>
> See you soon,
> 'Ossie'

However, despite this minor legalistic setback, don't you kids and grandkids worry too much about your inheritance. Nana's working on it.

Today is the first day of the rest of my life and I am not hungover nor do I hope to be anytime soon.

I get up and take a long hot shower and wash my hair. I prepare myself a healthy breakfast of oat bran cereal and fresh banana slices. I take my vitamins and one Valium, just for good measure. It's a beautiful day outside and the blue sky is shining through the sparkling new kitchen window.

I keep the curtains drawn on the living-room's big picture window, however. The back yard feels like a big black cloud in my mind, and there is no use crying over spilt milk, especially now that I've decided to be more optimistically oriented from this day forward.

In a couple more days or so I will go out and do something productive. Like weeding or planting vegetables

57

in a tilled little garden, with the seed packets posted on tiny wooden stakes – just like I did with the children when they were growing up. By enacting positive accomplishments in my back yard I will gradually dispel the idea of the black cloud. I will make my environment sunnier, brighter, and more life-affirming.

Until I'm ready to do something positive about my gardening environment, however, I'd just as soon not think about it.

I put on my white blouse with the lacy collar. I put on my green skirt and give myself another rousing pep talk.

Okay, Emma, so you were never a great beauty. But you have only improved with age. You still have a pretty remarkable figure considering you never exercised properly and, surprisingly enough, gray hair looks really good on you. A little make-up wouldn't hurt, though. And maybe a little of that white tooth polish when you brush.

Then I spray myself with Chanel, which my daughter-in-law sent me years ago for my birthday. That was before she began having children of her own, however, and both her and Thomas started forgetting my birthday practically every year, not even a card or anything. Almost like clockwork.

Probably no big deal in the Universal Scheme of Development and all that. But since it was the only birthday card I ever received except the one from the dry cleaners (who always included a 10% OFF discount certificate) it was sorely missed.

Over and over again I hear a beautiful song that comes out of nowhere. I am singing it in the back of my mind at first, but then I start singing it out loud in my big empty house, with all the windows open (except the picture window) and letting the whole world look in at me, what do I care:

> You don't have to say you love me
> Just because I'm near.
> You don't have to stay forever,
> Just hold tight, my dear.

Which are all the lyrics I remember, so I sing them over and over to myself without any break. They are so beautiful I catch myself starting to cry at one point, and it seems so silly, since I'm not thinking about my life, only how sad and beautiful the song sounds.

While I warm up the Oldsmobile in the garage I go out to the front yard and pick up some stray newspapers and candy wrappers that the wind has blown around. I am being careful on account of my back when who else but Officer Rodrigues comes driving by in his powerful black and white police car.

'Good morning, Mrs O'Hallahan,' he says. He is a very handsome young man when he smiles and I can see there is something different about his uniform. More solid-looking and self-assured.

'Why, good morning, dear. Where's your friend, the other police officer?' I look at him for a moment and feel a little displaced, like a moment of time has been snatched out from under me. I look at the bits of trash in my hand.

'You mean Officer Lathrop,' Officer Rodrigues tells me. 'He's been reassigned, now that I don't need a training partner anymore. Which leaves me on my own, doing a little house-to-house. I guess our friend Estelle Stansfield still hasn't shown her pointy little face around here, huh?'

I twist the trash into a big wad and try hiding it behind my back. Then I slip it into the side pocket of my sweater.

'I guess not, Officer Rodrigues. But I'm sure she'll show up eventually. Meanwhile, how would you like a sandwich? I'm on my way into town, but I'm sure I have time to fix you a little snack.'

Officer Rodrigues looks past me towards my kitchen, then at my Oldsmobile warming up in the garage. He seems very sad to see the engine ratcheting away and oily smoke rolling out of it like toast igniting in a bad toaster.

'No, I guess not, Emma,' he says sadly. Then, momentarily, he brightens a little. 'But maybe next time – okay?'

12

I go into town looking for something but I don't know what. I have all this deep energy inside my body and can't sit still even while I'm driving. I go to Ralph's and buy lots of fresh produce. Green vegetables, canned sweet corn, garlic, cheese croutons, and lo-cal Paul Newman Italian salad dressing. But right away I know none of that's what I'm looking for.

I buy sacks of red winesap apples, a few rusty-looking pears, and some hard greenish bananas, because fresh fruit every day helps balance out your emotional conflicts.

But no, I realize. Fresh fruit isn't it.

I pass the liquor aisle and see my favorite brandy, but I don't buy any. This *might* be what I'm looking for, since I start to feel very irritable with myself when I pass it, and all sorts of anger flares up in me about Marvin ruining my life and so on. But I don't think that's what I'm looking for, either.

I buy some ladies magazines and one Kit-Kat bar (just because I'm going to be health-conscious doesn't mean I have to go *overboard* or anything.) But that's not it, either. I'm stumped.

So I stand in the checkout line and read one of my magazines. The article I read is about women who have orgasms while riding in their cars! (So *that's* how it works, I tell myself.) Then I skip through the article to see if any of these attractive young models drive '67 Oldsmobiles, but apparently they don't.

Funny enough, this magazine article has affected me strangely, making me forget about the brandy I didn't buy, or the Kit-Kat bar I did. I get this strange tingling sensation in my toes, which travels up the backs of my legs and into the nape of my neck. I start up my Oldsmobile in the Ralph's parking lot but I don't want to go anywhere. Suddenly I feel at home in my own body, which is a very weird sensation to have in a Ralph's parking lot. I just want to sit here inside myself and maybe take a long nap.

I never had any orgasms in a car but during the late sixties I think I had a series of orgasms while watching the Mike Douglas TV Show, a ninety-minute talk and variety program which aired every afternoon at two p.m. In retrospect I know it probably sounds pretty embarrassing and ridiculous to think of your ugly old grandma having orgasms, but I've promised to be truthful from now on so here goes.

During the late sixties was like the last period of relative happiness I ever knew before I shot your grandpa. Marvin was still working at Consolidated Mutual in Anaheim, where he drove early every morning and didn't get home until seven or eight p.m. You kids had either run away from home or gone to college, and ever since your grandpa went to the local Neighborhood Action Committee and threatened to blow anybody's head off who tried to break into our canned goods in the event of nuclear war, I was pretty much left on my lonesome by the local populace. This meant all I had left to do anymore was work hard cleaning and gardening, making the beds and picking up every bit of stray dust or lint to keep your grandpa satisfied.

But we all find our happiness where we can, I guess, and I found mine just when I needed it. Every day at two p.m. I would sit down for a glass of brandy with my old friend, Mike Douglas, and know I wouldn't be interrupted by anybody for the entire next hour and a half. It was a very warm secure feeling, and the only real privacy I knew during that horrible decade. I know most people remember the sixties as a period of anti-war marches (which I agreed with but never had time or courage enough to support), LSD 'trips' and 'freak-outs', *Dragnet*, black protests, free love and Watergate, but I personally still remember it as the decade of Mike Douglas.

Mike Douglas was like a family to me after you kids moved out. He was always in a very cheery mood, making jokes all the time, and while his jokes weren't brilliant or anything I didn't really need a comic genius to keep me entertained. He also had many funny comedians from Lake Tahoe and Reno, Nevada, and a few song-stylists like Steve and Edie or Jack Jones or these two handsome men who sang duets in French and English together. But then late in the show Mike and his other guests (and his guest-host, who spent the week with Mike cooking up favorite recipes, and talking about how successful his or her marriage was even though they made lots of nasty jokes about it) would grow very solemn. At this point a serious guest would come out, usually the author of a new bestselling book, or a former celebrity involved with helping the sufferers of some life-threatening disease like polio or gangrene or even worse. Human sexuality was often the subject of these serious discussions, and since it always came at the end of the show I was feeling pretty cozy by then. I would be drinking my third jigger of brandy and Mike would get this very squinty expression on his face (kind of like a cute little basset hound) whenever he asked a question. At first I thought he got very sad whenever he discussed serious issues, but then I began to realize he was just having trouble reading those damn cue cards.

'A lot of people were raised to think human sexuality is something to be ashamed of,' Mike might say. 'But is sex education in the schools a valid solution to this problem?'

Or: 'How does a parent explain to his or her child that sexuality and loving are not two entirely different things?'

Or: 'What is the *proper* role of sexuality in today's

'permissive' and 'youth-oriented' (i.e. for Mike this meant 'totally sex-crazed' and 'communistical') society?'

Mike's serious guest, usually a bearded man with a Ph.D. in psychology or education, would answer all of Mike's questions with loads of personal self-assurance. He was so confident there were firm normal answers to these rather titillating questions that the audience, which was mainly hopeless old ladies like myself, breathed a collective sigh of relief. I think there were times in that decade when us older ladies were starting to feel as if the entire cockeyed world was going completely out of control. Everybody was having sex but us and there was nothing we could do about it.

Funny thing is that while Mike and his guests were discussing the serious aspects of sexuality I kept getting this tingling sensation in the back of my legs. In fact all I could think about was this soft blue cloud of everything that *wasn't* serious about human sexuality. It was the soft blue cloud of everything I didn't know and hadn't ever done. I would rest my hands in my lap or smooth out my dress. I would loosen a button on my blouse and open a window to catch the afternoon breeze. My house seemed really big and empty and I knew nobody would be coming by until long after the show was finished. I felt a little out of breath. When I touched my knee the tingling sensation sort of buzzed a little. I heard it in my ears. My spine tingled, my face. And then, since nobody was around, I didn't really, well, but then, I guess I sort of *did* . . .

At the end of the discussion on human sexuality the guest comedian that day would make a crazy joke like: 'After all this talk about sex, Mike, I don't know about you – but *I* need a cigarette!' Then he'd light up like three or four cigarettes and his hand would be shaking and we'd all laugh, kind with relief.

Some Mike Douglas shows were better than others but all of them were pretty good.

And that was pretty much my last concerted period of thinking about sexuality during my 'middle-aged' years.

Until the parking lot at Ralph's, that is.

*

63

When I was young I may have been the only girl on my block who didn't know anything about human sexuality. In retrospect I now know that not only did most of the other children my age *know* about sex, but many were actually *performing* it, one way or another, at every possible opportunity. Good for them.

When I was in my developing years I lived with my parents and my sister, Sophie, in San Pedro, where my father loaded and unloaded military equipment during the war as a longshoreman with Local 339. In high school my sister, who was a year younger than me, used to have other boys and girls over to our house for 'blackout' parties. Our house was usually empty, since our mother was always out drinking at bars, and our father usually worked nights or was drinking at different bars than our mother did (mainly because they didn't get along very well). Our mother was a full-time drunk, but our father was a hardworking man who was only drunk in his spare time. This personality difference led to many marital conflicts, until eventually there wasn't much marriage left, I'm afraid. Divorce wasn't an option for solving marital problems in those days, so basically people just stayed together ad infinitum until they made each other (and their children) totally miserable.

Blackout parties were when my sister and her friends would race around the house screaming like idiots and one of them, usually a retarded-looking, carroty Irish boy named Jimmy Lynch, would stand outside near the switch box and shut off all the lights suddenly. It was like practicing for the real blackouts we had in San Pedro all the time, since the Japanese were planning to destroy our naval station which was crucial to the defense of the Western Seaboard, or something crazy like that.

During each 'blackout', the entire house would go very quiet. Everybody would stop running and screaming and hide in whatever room they were in. I used to sit in the living room in the stuffed chair with my book and look at the moon outside, or the lights from the wharf. I would pretend I was walking down the white streets in a flowing white silk robe, like Grace Kelly or Rita Hayworth. I could hear people breathing in the house around me. I thought they were thinking about the white streets too. I thought they were imagining what it would be like to wander the white streets forever and never have to go back to a home where all people ever did was fight and drink all the time.

Little did I know they were probably having sex with one another!

Boy, was I surprised when Sophie told me.

'Why don't you loosen up and have some fun, Emma?' she would ask me, but I never understood what she meant. Because when the 'blackouts' occurred and all the lights went out I thought I *was* 'loosening up' and 'having fun'. I was hiding in the darkness in my soft chair with my book in my arms. I was wandering away from my body and home and never coming back. I felt this funny lifting sensation in my face and my chest, reminding me of all the places I had never been or would never be again. I called this sensation 'homesickness', the feeling that even though I was very far away from where I truly belonged, that at least I *did* have a *memory* of belonging, which was better than no sense of belonging at all. I even felt the tingling sensation in my face and down the insides of my legs, sort of my own private version of sexuality, I guess.

Because for me, you see, sex was always something I imagined, even when I didn't know what it was. Like the landscapes in books or the music on record albums.

On my way home I stop at my Savings and Loan, which is filled with various investors, policemen, security guards and so on. Everybody is yelling at everybody else, and a fleet of strange, anonymous-looking men in beige suits are behind the teller-booths and counting up gray stacks of money. They are taking big brown boxes out of the back rooms on rolling steel gurneys. They have placed some sort of red and white striped tape over the bank vault and when they close up the various tills they tape those over, too.

Mr Sullivan is standing in the sun and smiling optimistically as per usual. He is standing over near the front window with some of the other tellers and customers.

'Aye and begorrah,' he tells me. 'If it ain't be the lovely Mrs O'Hallahan comin' to visit.'

I'm so nervous my whole face feels cottony. I can't see anywhere in my peripheral vision. Mr Sullivan's face looks far away, as if I'm looking at him through the wrong end of a telescope.

Without thinking, I hand him my social security check. I haven't even endorsed it or anything.

Mr Sullivan is still smiling, but now he does it very sadly. He stops using his stupid Irish brogue.

'And here you just opened your own savings account,' he tells my social security check. 'And six weeks later we've gone into foreclosure on account of the crooked government.'

'That's okay, Mr Sullivan,' I tell him.

I don't know what foreclosure means, but if it means I lost my miserable few hundred dollars or so, then I've got bigger fish to fry. I feel the warm shapes of the other tellers and customers standing around. They're talking to each other but I'm sure they're staring straight at me.

'I have plenty of savings put away in a safe place, so don't worry about me,' I tell him. 'In fact, I didn't come by to ask about my stupid savings account. I came by to ask you to dinner.'

13

Even though we only started talking together at the Savings and Loan about a year ago, Mr Sullivan and I have shared many coincidental events in our lives. We were both married in a leap year. We both like sun-tea with lemon. We both had ungrateful spouses who took us for granted before their sudden demises, and two children apiece, and all our children have grandkids. Mr Sullivan is a Leo and I'm a Virgo, which come right after each other on all the astrological charts. Both of us were severely disappointed by Halley's comet, especially since neither of us will be around to see it next time.

I have started drinking brandy even before Mr Sullivan gets here. It has been two days since I saw him at the Savings and Loan (which, incidentally, is now the subject of many very boring local TV news stories). I know I made a promise to myself to lay off the brandy, but this is my first date in something like fifty years, so I probably owe myself a favor. And, speaking of dates, the *last* time I went on one was with Marvin, who I'm sorry to say I went ahead and married anyway. Whoops.

So as you can see: past experiences don't exactly leave me with a very favorable dating-impression.

'Here we go again,' Marvin says. He is sitting in the living room on the stuffed chair, watching his hero Patrick Buchanan on *Crossfire*. 'Blame Marvin for *everything*.' Then Marvin goes back to staring at Patrick Buchanan, who's arguing there's only one solution to the rapidly expanding crime problem in America. Harsher prison sentences and the death penalty.

'Damn right,' Marvin says, clenching his fists on the armrests.

By this time I'm ready to dig a new hole in the garden just for Mr Buchanan. I will put it right next to Marvin so they can sit out there agreeing with each other all the time and filling up with more and more blood pressure just like big fat angry balloons.

I take my brandy into the living room and stand right between Marvin and the TV. Marvin, though, keeps staring at the TV and pulling his lower lip, as if I'm the one who's the ghost and he's not.

'You just keep your stupid mouth shut, Marvin,' I tell him right off. I used to sit and take Marvin's guff hour after hour and day after day, and it would leave me feeling angry for weeks. But now that he's dead I fire right back at him immediately, since I'm not in the mood for any of his nonsense. 'I don't want you interrupting anything when my friend Mr Sullivan gets here. Or maybe you'd like me to hammer a few more steel poles into you. How'd you like *that*, Mr Tougher Law Enforcement Procedures?'

Marvin places one hand over his chest and winces, as if his heartburn's acting up again. He is totally filthy with dirt and gray, tangled roots all over him. There are worms in his hair, and some sort of pale sluggish mushroom growing on the right side of his face.

'If I were you, Emma,' he says, 'I'd take a look at what's happening in our back garden.'

That's Marvin's favorite gambit. The 'change the subject' gambit.

I tell him, 'I'll take care of the back garden when I damn well feel like it, *Marvin*. And not a minute sooner.'

'You better take care of the back garden, Emma. Or one of these days the back garden's going to take care of you.'

I'm so furious I can't see straight. I go to the kitchen, pour myself another brandy and take another Valium (of which I suddenly realize I've almost finished this prescrip-

68

tion already). Then I march right back into the living room to give Marvin another piece of my mind before I forget what it is I'm angry about. That's Marvin's trick, you see. He keeps insinuating all these terrible things about your looks and intelligence so you're never *exactly* certain what sorts of things he's *actually* saying. So then you completely forget what got you mad in the first place and you wander around all day with this terrible anger in you, getting hotter and hotter. Eventually you start thinking in an irrational manner and behaving just like our friend Patrick Buchanan.

This time, though, I won't let him get away with it.

'If you *really* cared about the condition of our back garden,' I yell, 'then maybe you'd have helped out a little more over the years, doing some of the mowing and the weeding, and not just making racial insults to all our nice gardeners about being Chinese or Mexican.'

Boy, I've hardly started yet. I feel like I've tapped a good solid vein which will provide me hours of serious yelling at Marvin.

'And *another* thing, *Marv*in,' I shout. I stomp into the living room and stand in front of his TV again.

But of course I should have figured. Marvin isn't there anymore.

There's a cup of cold coffee on the TV tray beside the stuffed chair. A weird configuration of stale cream is blossoming in it.

'We're talking about a lot of phoney hankie-waving, sap-mongering, mushy-mouthed liberal sentiment,' Patrick Buchanan is saying. 'And if liberals want to sympathize with the criminal community so much then maybe they should try spending a night alone in Watts or Harlem without our brave men in blue out there to protect them. Maybe we'd see how much sympathizing with the so-called underclass they'd be willing to do *then*.'

Much like Marvin, stupid old Patrick Buchanan never lets me get the last word in on *anything*.

'Shut up, Patrick,' I say, without even looking at his fat piggy face.

Then I shut off the TV with the remote control. And that's where I'm standing when Mr Sullivan rings the front doorbell.

Even though I have a lovely dinner with Mr Sullivan, all I can think about for the rest of the evening is the back garden and what might be out there.

'This is a delicious pot-roast, Emma,' Mr Sullivan says. Mr Sullivan is wearing a nicely ironed white linen shirt and a blue silk tie. He is wearing cotton trousers and polished cordovan leather shoes. I don't think I've ever sat down to dinner with a man this well-dressed in my entire life. He has even combed his hair.

'And the peas and carrots,' he says. Mr Sullivan indicates them with his fork. He finishes chewing and swallows. 'Yum.'

Personally I'm having trouble with the digestion-aspect of my food. I keep imagining all sorts of god-forsaken catastrophes out there in my back garden. Enormous trees have sprouted from the ground, bearing the rotted corpses of your grandpa and Mrs Stansfield in their branches for all the world to see. Or wild cats pulling them from the ground and cracking the broken bones between their teeth, sucking out the yellow marrow, then getting hairballs and retching all over everything. Or the yard being littered with human fingernails and eyeballs. I even imagine the dead bodies revived by voodoo magic, all bony and smelly, staggering around the yard and bumping into the wooden fences, like on those horrible movies that used to keep me awake half the night on *Creature Features*.

Marvin and Mrs Stansfield. Mrs Stansfield and Marvin.

All through the meal I keep looking over my shoulder at the curtains across the picture window. The moon is glowing through like a big streetlamp. I know it's just my overactive imagination but that doesn't make me feel any better. I drink my brandy without looking at Mr Sullivan. I want something stronger than brandy but I don't know what.

70

'Here's looking at you, Emma,' Mr Sullivan says. He's smiling at me through the bell-shaped, long-stemmed wine glass I gave him to drink his mineral water with.

This is like the thousandth salute Mr Sullivan has toasted me with since he got here.

It's a good excuse for another sip of brandy, though.

'You know, Mr Sullivan,' I tell him, 'I'm very sorry I'm not myself this evening. I think I may be coming down with a flu or something.'

Mr Sullivan winks at me. 'I certainly couldn't tell it from looking at you, Emma. I must say you're looking especially *lovely* this evening.'

I am thinking that Mr Sullivan, who is very charming in two to three minute intervals at the Savings and Loan, can be a bit too much to take in longer doses.

'That's very sweet of you to say, Mr Sullivan.' I hand him the plate of pork chops. 'Now, why don't you have some more meat.'

'I'd *love* some more meat.' Mr Sullivan gives me that flirty wink of his. But I can't work up enough attention span to flirt back since I'm already staring at the curtains again.

Mr Sullivan forks more pork chops onto his plate. Then he follows my gaze to the picture window, then back to me again, as if he's hanging clothes on a clothes-line.

'Perhaps we should take our aperitifs into the back garden,' Mr Sullivan says. 'We could sit together under the stars and get better acquainted.'

Oh, boy – isn't life pitiful? Here I've been dreaming for ages about getting Mr Sullivan into my house and now all I want is to get rid of him!

'Hoo boy,' I tell Mr Sullivan. I wipe my napkin across my forehead really slow, hoping I'll draw his attention away from my eyes. 'I feel like I'm burning up. Maybe we could do this another time, Mr Sullivan. I really should try hitting the hay pretty early tonight.'

Mr Sullivan smiles that little smile again. Then he runs his fingers through his glistening gray hair.

'I feel the same fever, Emma,' he says. He toasts me silently with the Perrier-filled wine glass. His eyes are sparkling too. 'I feel it every time we're together.'

I offer Mr Sullivan more rice. I offer him more peas, carrots, and apple sauce for his pork chops.

'No, thank you,' Mr Sullivan keeps telling me. Finally I realize I'm in the middle of my usual denial-mechanism behavior pattern. I want to ask Mr Sullivan something important, but instead of coming right out with it I'm trying to bury him (pardon the expression) under a lot of extra food and services he doesn't require. It's like I'm apologizing really hard for the fact I *want* to speak honestly to him.

Here's some more peas, carrots, meat, dairy products and dessert, Mr Sullivan. I'm sure you'd rather have me pouring food onto your plate than opening my big fat mouth.

Poor screwed-up old Emma, I think.

Finally, I can't stand being myself anymore. I have to be someone else. I have to be someone who grabs life by the horns and damns the consequences.

'Mr Sullivan,' I ask right out loud, 'would you mind if I asked you a personal question?'

Mr Sullivan's head is still pointed in my direction, but his gaze has turned inward.

'What's that, Emma?'

I feel a little dizzy and overheated. I lean across the table. I open my big fat mouth.

'When your wife Doris passed away of coronary thrombosis, did you miss her? I mean, I know she didn't treat you very nicely, and she made you push her around in a wheelchair even though she wasn't crippled. But even though you may not have liked her very much, did you still miss her when she was gone? Did you still hear her voice in your head and see her face? Did you ever think that maybe, just maybe, she wasn't so horrible after all, and that maybe there was something horrible with *you* that kind of latched onto her, and made her mean and nasty because that was the only way she could cope with *your* horribleness and bad faith? Do you ever think about things like that, Mr Sullivan? I mean, I guess all I'm asking is: Do you ever feel any regrets about your wife Doris being dead?'

I'm all out of breath and fluttery, and the entire house has grown incredibly still. Mr Sullivan's expression is very unfocused and distant, gazing at the curtains of the picture window and wondering what's out there.

'Actually,' Mr Sullivan says, and wipes his lips with the white cloth napkin, 'I don't have any regrets about poor Doris. Maybe I *wish* I did. But I don't.'

That night after I get rid of Mr Sullivan I do all the washing-up in the kitchen, even though the brandy has made me very wobbly. I can only concentrate on one thing at a time. The dishes, the sink, hot water in the sink, a glass of cool water, a handful of aspirin. At one point I leave the water running in the sink and it starts spilling onto the floor before I turn it off. Then I see the mop. The Saran Wrap. The refrigerator-freezer. It's very dark outside the kitchen window. I can feel the weight out there, all humid and muggy.

Waiting. Definitely waiting.

I sit down at the kitchen table. The pork chops are drying on a plate, bellying upward.

'It's time,' Marvin says in the living room. 'It's time.'

During the Cuban Missile Crisis Marvin started bringing home all sorts of magazines about building your own bomb shelter. He talked about digging an enormous hole in our back yard and lining it with tar paper and concrete. Our bomb shelter would be equipped with a ham radio, a chemical toilet, two sets of bunkbeds from the Army Navy store, and many cases of Sterno. Marvin began storing tons of canned goods in the linen closet, freeze-dried meat and bottled water. In case of thermonuclear war, Marvin claimed that we and the two kids were supposed to climb down into the bomb shelter for seven weeks until the radiation died down. We would have to bring all our guns and ammunition with us because our neighbors would kill us if they could, fighting over control of the bomb shelter for the salvation of their loved ones. When we came out again in seven weeks the entire world would be totally changed and we would be forced to propagate our species across the surface of our ruined planet. The idea that the propagation of our species would be left up to me and Marvin, as well as our two very disturbed children, Tony and Cassie, used to make me so sick with worrying that I vomited on several occasions.

(If I had *my* choice, the world outside would stay just the way it is and *I* would climb down into the bomb shelter and lock the door behind me. And nobody would ever notice the difference.)

Then, when the Cuban Missile Crisis died down, Marvin wanted to pave the back yard over with concrete and gravel, so we wouldn't have to do any weeding. But I insisted on a garden and I never regretted it until tonight.

I go to the picture window and pull back the curtain a little. It's totally dark outside. All I can see is the glare of my own reflection in the window and Marvin sitting in the stuffed chair behind me. There's a darker, leaner shadow on the sofa, but I can't quite make it out.

'Go take a look, Emma,' Mrs Stansfield says. I'd recognize her voice anywhere. 'It's time you started taking responsibility for your actions.'

I know, Mrs Stansfield.

I unlatch the picture window and pull it open. It screaks on rusty casters. I hear the frogs down at the creek and the wheezing of crickets. I flick on the porch light.

All these eyes looking at me. Spiders, crickets, newts in the birdbath, lizards, owls. I never noticed how many animals are in that tiny yard just looking at you. Everything is green and overgrown, with weeds climbing out of fissures in the concrete porch. Then I look at the various shapes of discolored dirt. I see the places I dug for the savings account, Marvin, and Mrs Stansfield. They are very clearly defined, like different colored squares on a Monopoly board.

Then I see another long, rectangular shape of discolored dirt, situated right next to Mrs Stansfield's place near the

74

back fence. It looks about the same length as Mrs Stansfield. But it looks a lot shallower, too.

Let me see. Marvin, Mrs Stansfield, the savings account. One, two, three.

But when I include the rectangular shape near the back fence, my numbering goes all out of whack.

One, two, three, four.

Grave number four is not such a nice job and was obviously done in a much bigger hurry than the others.

Uh-oh, Emma, I think.

Uh-oh.

14

This time I don't mind my hangover that much – at least it keeps my brain occupied. All I keep thinking is hangover. Hangover. Hangover. My whole body is throbbing into my head and I feel too sick to be depressed. Thank goodness for small miracles.

I take a long cold shower. I go downstairs.

The curtain is still open on the picture window. In the daytime Marvin's grave isn't so pronounced anymore. The dirt is changing color and beginning to look like the rest of the gardening area. The other graves, including the place where I buried the savings account, are still very distinct, though.

One, two, three, four.

Then I count them again, just to make sure.

I fix my healthy breakfast, consisting of oat bran cereal and an apple. I am going to try to do better this time with my diet. I drink black coffee and take my vitamins.

Marvin, meanwhile, is having toast with cherry jam. The big white mushroom on the side of his head has begun to deflate. It's not much of an improvement, though.

'I used the last of the cherry jam,' Marvin says. He chews noisily and slurps his coffee.

I go upstairs to my office and write in this journal for a little while. Then I take out a clean sheet of white paper and write at the top:

PEOPLE WHO MAY BE BURIED IN THE
BACK GARDEN

Then I try coming up with a list of possibilities. Ibid.

1. The mailman.
2. The meter reader.
3. Jack the insurance man.
4. Dave the milkman.
5. A Jehovah's Witness.
6. Nobody (i.e. I just dug the hole and filled it in during a period of especially bad derangement). (P.S. I wish.)
7.

After I get to number seven I can't think of anybody else, so I sit at my desk for a good long think. I hear the TV blaring downstairs in the living room. I start thinking hangover. Hangover. Hangover. There is somebody whose name I don't want to write at the bottom of my list, but I can't seem to remember who it is.

I look at my other list pinned to the billboard:

WHAT'S WRONG WITH AMERICA

There are spaces left on this list too.
Oh my.

Before I fix my lunch I take down the Remington 700 rifle from Marvin's gun collection. Marvin bought the Remington when he went to the *Guns and Survival Magazine* tactical competition in Orange County last year. (I'm afraid he only went for the afternoon though I encouraged him to spend the entire weekend. Fat chance.)

Marvin came back from this wonderful competition with the Remington because, in his words, 'Crisis-control experts these days spend too much time on door-entry techniques and not enough time on long range rifle tactics. I don't want *us* to fall into that trap.'

So Marvin took me to the firing range and taught me

how to use the rifle as well as the handguns. This was back when Marvin's doctor said he was suffering from an embolism, from which he could be attacked at any moment. In the event that Marvin suffered an embolism and became bedridden it would be up to me to protect our home from the wildly mutating inner-city hordes who would try making serious life-threatening incursions into our personal-living-arena.

So about the most educational thing that ever happened to me was the result of an embolism in Marvin. Makes sense.

When I carry the rifle through the living room Marvin is watching *Divorce Court* on TV and brushing Pringles crumbs off his chest. When I go by with the rifle he looks up.

'Where do you think you're going with that?' he asks.

I take the Remington into the back yard where it is sunny as always. The birds are chirping away and I say, 'Sorry, birds.' Then I fire about a dozen rounds of Federal 168 grain boattail hollowpoint into Marvin's grave. The gun recoils against my shoulder with a *whufft!*, *whufft!*, *whufft!* The bullets leave thick impact holes in Marvin's grave, and one of them even reveals a bit of Marvin's gray flannel shirt. I kick loose dirt over the holes with my feet.

I stand for a while with the rifle and listen. I think I hear a distant, high-pitched hissing sound, like air being let out of a tire.

After a while the hissing sound turns into the absence of birds. And then, after another long moment, I hear the scrape of a window next door, in a house filled with people I've never met. The window makes a hard clunking sound when it closes. It's a sound that makes me feel very alone and thoughtful. I am aware of a deep sadness I haven't been allowing myself to feel for weeks. It's not a sadness about Marvin or even Mrs Stansfield because it's totally selfish and makes me feel completely alone.

When I take the Remington back inside the TV is still on and there are Pringles all over Marvin's chair. But no Marvin.

Bingo.

I take the rifle upstairs and put it back in the gun case. Then I sit down at my desk with the two uncompleted lists I've been working on.

At the bottom of the list entitled WHAT'S WRONG WITH AMERICA I write:

8. You can rifle more than a dozen rounds into your dead husband's grave in your back yard and nobody even bothers to call the police anymore.

Then I pin that list back on the bulletin board and take down the other one. At the bottom of the list entitled PEOPLE WHO MAY BE BURIED IN THE BACK GARDEN I write:

7. My poor naive unknowing grandson, Teddy.

Then I go downstairs and fix myself a nice healthy salad for lunch.

After lunch I call Mr Sullivan's house and the phone rings about ten times. On the eleventh ring, however, Mr Sullivan picks up the phone and says, 'Hello?'

Thank God, I think. Then I hang up.

I have been reading over my journal (something I promised myself I wouldn't do) and have just reached the end of describing my dinner date with Mr Sullivan. At the part where I said, 'All I want is to get rid of him' I took a terrible gasp of breath and felt a cold slippery sensation in my bowels.

But obviously Mr Sullivan arrived home safely so that's at least one name I won't have to add to my list.

I sit in the lawn chair in the back yard for a while. I fold up my dress to my waist and slip off the shoulder straps. Then I bake in the sun and try not to worry about anything important, just enjoying the moment the best I can.

But I can't help thinking: What a lousy grandma.

Talk about bad positive role models! Not only are you hearing about your husband-murdering Nana but maybe even a Nana who bloodily kills her own unfortunate offspring. I swear there are days when I don't understand anything, especially my own life.

But then I cheer myself up by realizing all this worrying about grandson Teddy is nonsense. Just because I've been suffering memory lapses doesn't make me insane, does it? I mean, even if I forget things, I'm still the same person I always was, even if I *don't* remember every single thing I've ever done. Even the terrible things I *know* I've done don't make me feel very sorry or apologetic, whereas killing my own grandchild would definitely make me feel *really* sorry.

In fact, I can't imagine any situations, no matter how preposterous, in which I'd seriously contemplate murdering one of my own grandkids. (Well, not *many*, that is.)

By the time I'm finished giving myself a good talking to I feel a little better. I even sit up in my chair and take a look at the new grave next to Mrs Stansfield. Everything seems perfectly clear and ordinary in the strong white sunlight. There is still plenty of room out here in the garden, and I have loads of money, and there's a pretty good chance that I haven't killed Teddy (or maybe if I did, he even had it coming). I don't feel so scared or confused anymore, or like some crazy sociopathic freak.

Even when life gets pretty ridiculous, there's something extremely ordinary about it at the same time.

For instance, while I'm sitting here wondering who may or may not be buried in the garden and how they may or may not be related to me, something more important comes to mind.

I have to pee really bad.

So I march into the house and do just that.

15

That night I don't drink any brandy. Instead, I fix soup and salad and try to watch the CBS Evening News with Dan Rather. Watching the CBS Evening News means catching up with world affairs, something I've never been especially keen on. Tonight good old world affairs consists of the following items.

On the domestic scene: People without homes. People without jobs. People without a proper education. People who don't remember to vote, who don't care to vote, and who wouldn't vote even if they knew how. People who've given up. People who haven't given up, but the system has given up on them.

On the international scene: People in prisons and death camps. People shot by guerrillas and freedom fighters. People without arms and legs, sometimes just young girls, because other people are blowing them up with high-priced weaponry. People who make these high-priced weaponry with my hard-earned tax-money, and who pay large sums to congressmen and senators to help get them re-elected, who then give enormous amounts of money right back to the defense industry to buy a lot more overpriced weaponry.

And by this point, of course, the news has hardly begun.

People on drugs, the President telling people not to take drugs. People in prison, millions and millions of them. Drug dealers in South America who used to work for the

CIA, or who still work for the CIA, or who are looking for work with the CIA, which, like the horrible prisons, is about the only financially solvent organization in America (unlike the schools, or the hospitals, or the public transportation).

It is growing perfectly obvious (at least to me) that if there is a god, he has given mankind intelligence as a sort of cosmic joke. By building civilizations, men and women screw everything up so bad they destroy themselves in the process.

This is kind of like my philosophy of the universe, which I have tried not to bore you with too much so far, but which goes a little as follows:

First there is Cosmic Being and then there is Cosmic Non-Being. Cosmic Being builds things like shopping malls, auto- and steel-manufacturing plants, governmental bureaucracies, the Democratic Party, H.U.D., Van Nuys, the Department of Motor Vehicles, the United Nations, rock videos and bomb shelters. But in order to build new things, Cosmic Being has to take old things apart for the basic materials, and sometimes even kill them. Which is why we have strip-mining, the Nuclear Weapons Industry, AIDS, cancer, Washington lobbyists, supply-side economics, Ted Koppel, the *New York Times*, petrochemicals, maggots, vultures, worms and other assorted parasites. While Being builds everything up, Non-Being tears everything down. And just as it's impossible to conceive of building something up without the simultaneous idea of tearing something else down, the exact opposite is true also.

For example: In order to build my own private, happy world here in my house, I have had to do serious damage to at least two (and probably three) of my fellow human beings.

Meanwhile, my serious damage to these two or three human beings has contributed not only to my personal well-being, but to an eventual long-range improvement in my back-garden's fertility ratio.

In other words, I do not believe good and evil are

separate ideas like my ex-husband Marvin does. Instead, I believe the universe is a very confusing place to be, even on its best days.

So while the entire world is falling apart right in front of our eyes, Dan Rather decides to do a major news story on guess what pressing modern problem? The assassination of President Kennedy. And then, right in the middle of Dan's serious doubts about the Warren Commission Report, somebody rings my front doorbell.

See, that's what I mean by the strangely positive effects of what many people might consider my evil or destructive deeds.

I keep having so many unexpected visitors!

'I'm sorry to keep bothering you,' Officer Rodrigues says after his second slice of Sarah Lee frozen pound cake. 'But I'm afraid I've been called out here for the second evening in a row by your neighbor Mr Stansfield, who keeps complaining to my desk sargent about what he calls my "negligent law-enforcement procedures". Ever since the disappearance of his wife, your neighbor Mr Stansfield has become a big royal blue pain in the buttinski – if you'll pardon my French. And by the way, Emma, this pound cake is delicious.'

'I'm afraid it's still a little frozen in the center,' I tell him. 'If I'd known you were coming, I'd have baked a real cake.'

Officer Rodrigues sips my coffee with a far-away expression on his face. Officer Rodrigues is thinking about a place with white sandy beaches and blue, blue water, a place very far away from this boring suburb called Dynamo Valley. Beautiful blonde women are wind-surfing across the white-capped blue waves. Beautiful brown-skinned native girls in bikinis are serving him exotic drinks from coconut shells. Big-bosomed girls with beautiful white teeth.

'Sometimes a person just needs a little time to sit down and think,' I tell Officer Rodrigues. 'Without a bunch of morons complaining at him all the time.'

Slowly Officer Rodrigues's smile swims in from the blue water and glides straight into my kitchen. Suddenly he's smiling directly at me.

'That's so true, Emma,' he says.

After another cup of coffee he fills me in:

'Mrs Stansfield isn't in Florida with her mother. She's not in Arizona with her kids. She's not in Las Vegas playing slot machines. She's not even at the beautiful and luxurious Gold Coast Mall, where she hasn't been sighted in days. Mrs Stansfield, I conclude, is not on holiday. She's not lost in traffic. She's not shacked up at the local Motel 6 with the neighborhood fire department. I know this much because her car is still parked in her garage, none of her clothes or luggage is missing, and she hasn't made any surprise withdrawals from her savings account. Sound mysterious? Maybe, maybe not. What I've done, see, is made up a list of possibilities.'

Officer Rodrigues leans to one side and withdraws a blue loose-leaf notebook from his back pocket.

'Very good,' I encourage him. 'That's exactly how I keep *my* thoughts straight. Making lists.'

Officer Rodrigues clears his throat.

'So here are some possibilities,' he says. 'Mrs Stansfield has been kidnapped and held for ransom, only the kidnappers lost her street address and phone number. Mrs Stansfield ran away and joined the circus. Mrs Stansfield's real name is Katerina Ivanovna Rostropovich, an East European mole planted in the West during the Cold War who, now that the Cold War is over, has dashed back to her native homeland for all the free borscht she can eat. Mrs Stansfield never actually existed but is only a figment of our collective imagination. Mrs Stansfield imploded. Mrs Stansfield is hiding under her bed. Mrs Stansfield joined the Peace Corps, the Hare Krishna, or the Moonies – take your pick. Mrs Stansfield evaporated. Mrs Stansfield suffered a really bad identity crisis and now she doesn't have any identity left. Mrs Stansfield's disappearance was engineered by my former training partner, Office Lathrop, that white Anglo asshole, in order to prove to my department they shouldn't hire any more officers of Latino descent. Mrs Stansfield went away. Mrs Stansfield succumbed. Mrs Stansfield had second thoughts. Mrs Stansfield,' Officer Rodrigues says, slowly closing his notebook and staring off into the blue water again. 'Mrs Estelle Veronica Stansfield.'

Officer Rogrigues is such a handsome, industrious young man, I can't help feeling slightly attracted to him. I promise myself that if I surrender myself to anybody it will be to Officer Rodrigues.

(What a nice little feather that would be in his law-enforcement cap!)

'Maybe she was accidentally struck on the head and caught amnesia,' I tell him, trying to help. 'Like what happened to Lynn Saratoga Davenport, the youngest daughter of Boss Davenport, on my favourite afternoon serial, *Loving to Share*.'

Officer Rodrigues replaces the notebook in his back pocket.

'Try being serious for just one minute, Emma,' he says. His expression is drifting far away again.

'I *am* being serious,' I tell him.

'I hate them all,' Officer Rodrigues says in a dull, flat voice. 'Officer Lathrop, my desk sargent, Mr Stansfield, the whole monotonous bunch of Anglo-*bendejo*-jackasses.' He mutters something darkly to himself.

'Present company excepted,' he adds.

Officer Rodrigues presses his index finger against his white plate. Then he transports the imprinted pound-cake-crumbs to his mouth.

'If they hire a Latin or a female because of his or her race or sex, everybody calls it PC,' Officer Rodrigues tells the distant blue water and white sandy beaches. 'But if they hire yet another male Anglo asshole because of his race or sex, then it's just the same old racist-sexist horseshit.'

I sneak up on the refrigerator while Officer Rodrigues is busy feeling sorry for himself. I open the door. Then I open the door of the freezer.

'Guess what I've got?' I ask Officer Rodrigues.

Officer Rodrigues looks up.

'Is it Mrs Stansfield?' he asks me. 'Have you killed her, chopped her into little pieces and stuffed her in the freezer?'

'Of course not, silly.'

Then I show him.

'Frozen Kit-Kat bars,' I say.

16

That night I sit down and write a long letter to my severely estranged daughter Cassie.

Dear Cassie, I write:

How are you? I'm fine.

My grandson Teddy, who I'm sure has just decided to take a little extra-curricular excursion for a while, has yet to arrive. I hope this doesn't make you worry too excessively.

Children, as I know from personal experience, often get a lot of crazy notions in their heads. Take my first daughter, for example, one Cassandra Louise O'Hallahan.

Cassandra was easily my favourite family member, and when she was little we had great times together. We made Play-Doh, and baked cookies, and ran through the lawn sprinklers together. We watched Captain Stardust's cartoon hour every afternoon at four o'clock. We dressed dolls, went shopping, and told each other our weirdest dreams.

Cassandra's older brother had started school already so we had the entire house to ourselves during the day. Everything was magical during that period of our lives, and the days stretched out forever, filled with great adventures shared between mother and daughter. Cassandra had a great sense of humor, a totally wacky imagination and a wonderful disposition. She didn't cry or pout whenever she didn't get what she wanted – like her father, say, or her brother Thomas. And she liked helping her mother clean the dishes and vacuum the rugs.

Then, terrible things began to happen to this idyllic relationship. Little Cassandra started school, and every morning her mother walked her to the local bus stop. She made sure Cassandra's Jetsons lunch-box was filled with nutritious goodies. A fresh red apple or green pear, a Thermos full of orange juice, Frito Lay Fritos, Deviled Ham sandwiches with mayo and lettuce on fluffy white Wonderbread. Then Cassandra got on the bus and went to school.

At first little Cassandra came home in a rush and told her mother everything. About the games she played and the things she learned, about her new teachers and friends. Then mother and daughter would go into the kitchen and work on little Cassandra's various school projects. They glued sugar cubes in the shape of bridges and buildings, for example. Or they transformed empty egg and milk cartons into original works of art. Little Cassandra never knew how happy these projects made her poor mother!

But eventually Cassandra started to change. She became prone to long, awkward silences in her mother's company. Sometimes she gave her mother hard looks filled with resentment and bad vibrations, even though all her mother was trying to do was fix her sandwiches and cookies, or make her usual, foolish jokes. She cried whenever her mother tried to walk her to the bus stop, or suggested they go shopping together. There was something about her mother which made Cassandra deeply ashamed. And so they began spending less time together.

As Cassandra got older she began bringing girlfriends home. Cool sophisticated girls who prematurely wore too many fancy cosmetics and lacy underwear. Cassandra hardly talked to her mother at all anymore, especially during meal times. And during these meal times her mother could have used all the support she could get, since while she was serving her family pot roasts and stews and chicken fried steaks all she ever heard from her husband

and son were complaints and negative-sounding criticisms all the time.

'This meat is gristly,' they said.

Or: 'You put too much water in the orange juice.'

Or: 'Can't you sit still for one minute, Emma? You're making us *nervous*.'

When she was younger, Cassandra often rushed to her mother's defense. She told her brother and father off, saying things like: 'Well, make your own damn orange juice,' or, 'Don't you guys even know how to say thank you?' But as she got older, she just looked at her mother with less and less love and more and more loathing.

'Why do you take that from them?' she asked her mother in the kitchen one evening. Cassandra was very upset with her mother by this point and practically crying. 'Don't you realize they're treating you like dirt? You're not some stupid *mule*, Mom. You don't *owe* them anything. Don't you realize they don't care about you? You're just another pack animal to them. You're just another kitchen appliance. They have about as much love for you as, well, for the washer-dryer or the can opener. Is that what you want to be the rest of your life, Mom? Some sort of human can-opener?'

Meanwhile, her mother was filled with so much shame and embarrassment for herself! She couldn't admit (even to herself) that her daughter was totally correct.

'Your father and brother mean well,' she told her daughter. Or: 'Maybe I *did* put too much water in the orange juice. You know how absent-minded I get.' But whenever her mother apologized or tried to pretend nothing was wrong, her daughter got even more upset. Eventually Cassandra stopped getting mad at her mother. In fact, she hardly talked to her at all anymore.

And so Cassandra got older, and her mother began spending all her afternoons alone in the house. She drank brandy, read books and watched Mike Douglas and *Loving to Share*. The house filled up with more and more dark spaces. The dark spaces were eating her up, moving into her body somehow, traveling in her blood and stomach like a virus. Alone in the house all day, her mother cried and cried, or listened to music on the record player. Music that made her sad while she was drinking, or cheered her up when the sadness got too terrible. Don Ho, Dean Martin, Perry Como, Burl Ives or the Serendipity Singers. Records which her mother couldn't put on when the rest of the family was around because all they did was make fun of them, even though it wouldn't have cost them anything to respect one of her few pleasures in life.

'Boy, is the sap running strong tonight!' your miserable father used to say, the moment he got in the door. Then your father would totally ignore my music and go turn on TV to watch David Brinkley. Or on Sunday it was G.E. College Bowl, so he could make fun of all the college kids whenever they got an answer wrong.

'Errrrrp, clang-clang-clang!' your miserable father would shout. He practically jumped out of his chair it made him so happy. 'That's Puerto Rico, you dumb numbskull! Haven't you ever heard of a *territory* before, Mr Pimple-Face. What do you do all day at college, anyway? Pull your pud? Pinch your nipples? You four-eyed jerk-brain.'

When Cassandra brought her friends home, her mother fixed them sandwiches, soups and snacks. Cassandra and her friends were getting older. They wore crazy clothes that showed off their beautifully changing young bodies. It made her mother very happy, but her mother was too embarrassed to say anything which might have a sexual-sounding content.

'Why don't you put on the Emma-dippety Singers, Mom,' Cassandra used to ask her mother. Then she would exchange a quick glance with her friend across the table and they would both start giggling.

'What's that, honey?' her mother would ask. 'What would you like to hear?'

'You heard me, Mom,' Cassandra would say, getting all frosty like her father. 'The Serendipity Singers. Why don't you put them on the record player? They're so *boss*.'

Almost every afternoon for four years little Cassandra

played that joke on me about the Emma-Dippety Singers in front of her friends. And I never got mad at her, or let her know for one minute how much it broke my heart. Just like with your father and brother, I was treated bad all the time because I deserved it, and I didn't have the courage to stand up for myself or my convictions.

Eventually my daughter hated me more and more. She stopped cleaning her room or helping with the dishes. She stayed out late and didn't call. She brought boys home and made love with them downstairs in the living room and left condoms and birth control pills and marijuana butts and other drug paraphernalia lying around where she knew I'd find them, and whenever I tried to talk to her about growing up and the responsibilities of being a woman she used to say to me:

'Oh really, Mom? Since when did *you* ever understand anything about the responsibilities of being a woman?'

Then one day Cassandra quit high-school and ran away with her fifty-five-year-old boyfriend, Raoul Stevenson. And her mother never saw her daughter Cassandra ever again.

By the time I get to this point in the letter I have started bawling like a baby. My nose has gotten completely snotty and I can't even breathe right. I blow my nose into a big dish towel and pretty soon the dish towel is soaking wet with tears. It hurts so bad I completely surprise myself. To some extent I am slightly relieved. Because it hurts so much, it seems a lot more real than just about anything else that has happened to me in my entire crummy lifetime.

Finally I try sounding a little more brave at the end of my letter and say:

Anyway, this is just the story of how sorry I am for being a lousy mother, but I always tried to do my best, even though I might not have produced very good results. I still love you very much, though, and miss you all the time.

Love from your mother, however worthless.

P.S.   Don't worry about Teddy. I'm sure he'll turn up eventually.

Then I enclose a hundred dollar bill as per usual, put it into an envelope, lick it shut and put on a stamp.

This way I can't read the letter over again and chicken out.

After my good cry I take a long bath in the tub with a cup of hot tea to perk me up. My whole body feels exhausted and trembly, and that weird tingling sensation has returned to my legs and stomach. I feel like my body's being charged with a faint electric current. Oh Emma, I think. Oh oh.

I wash myself from top to bottom. I put on my sun-dress and my good white slip. I put on my perfume and do the best I can with my hair.

On the way out I mail my letter at the mailbox.

When I get to Mr Sullivan's it is almost eight-thirty and he opens the door wearing just his bathrobe and reading glasses.

'Why, Emma,' he says. He pats his hair and rearranges his amber terrycloth robe. He seems either flustered or flattered, even he doesn't know which. 'What a pleasant surprise.'

Behind him I see a Sylvester Stallone video playing on the TV. Sylvester is doing what he does best: blowing a bunch of evil-looking men away with high-tech weaponry. Bang bang bang.

There is a TV tray beside the stuffed chair and a TV dinner on the tray. There is also a very tempting-looking bottle of Seagram's 7 standing next to a short-stemmed brandy glass.

'Well, are you going to invite me in?' I ask. 'Or are you going to leave me standing out here all night?'

17

After one night with Mr Sullivan – which counts as just my second physical relationship with a man in my entire life (not counting Mike Douglas) I have come to a major conclusion. Bad love is better than no love at all. No kidding.

Well, not bad, exactly. Maybe just miscoordinated.

First off, Mr Sullivan made me incredibly nervous by paying me so much attention! I don't know how to explain it. He kept whispering his usual blarney in my ear about how beautiful I am and my figure etcetera, which flattered me completely, even though I *knew* it was bullshit. (Go figure.) And even worse, he was constantly petting and touching me *all over*. What a change from Marvin the Hog, who touched me as little as possible, and who got it over with as quickly as possible too. Marvin always performed sex as if it were a chore to be efficiently accomplished – that way you wouldn't have to do it again for a long time. Like clipping your toenails or waxing the car.

Second off, I'm afraid I reached the peak of my bathtub sexual-arousal experience in my car on the way over here, so everything that occurred afterwards was sort of anti-climactic. (Maybe that magazine article about auto-orgasms was right, even if it *didn't* mention Oldsmobiles.)

This last fact made it kind of awkward for me when Mr Sullivan asked if it was as good for me as it was for him. How could I tell him: 'Yes, but it was good for me on the car ride over here. Then it went progressively downhill.'

93

I tried to be polite, however. And frankly I *was* terribly grateful.

Mr Sullivan's is a ranch-style three bedroom with a big back yard, just like every other house in Dynamo Valley. In fact, it's almost identical to my house, only the back yard doesn't verge onto the creek like mine does, but onto somebody else's back yard.

Not so much privacy, I think.

'I've left the place almost exactly as it was when Doris was alive,' Mr Sullivan tells me. Mr Sullivan has pulled on his frayed terrycloth robe again. He has come from the bathroom where he just brushed his teeth and combed his hair for about the thousandth time since I got here. He smells like Listerine and whiskey. A combination which smells pretty nice, actually.

Doris's wheelchair sits in the corner of the bedroom staring at us. Big spoky eyes and a worn leather seat faded white from the repeated impact of Doris's fat lazy bottom.

There's a picture of Doris as a young woman in a frame on the bureau. All her old jewelry boxes, cosmetics, prescription medicines and perfumes are still lying around, gathering dust and this thick, sticky residue which seems to get on everything you own after a certain age. There is a music-box shaped like a Christmas tree, and a small mirrored serving tray with gold filigree.

The first chance I get I remove Mr Sullivan's hands from my person, sit up on the edge of the bed and lean towards the bureau to see Doris's picture a little better. Feeling bold for a moment, I even reach out and pick it up.

'She was very beautiful,' I say, which is absolutely true.

Doris's picture is from her early twenties. She has dark features and smoky brown eyes, like one of those femme fatales in the old black and white movies. Olive skin and pouty lips. She seems to be standing in a doorway or something, her arms folded, with a long angular shadow leaning behind her. Her black hair is tied up in a bun to reveal her thin shoulders in a low-cut black dress. It's a very arty photo, and the way Doris's smoky eyes look at you, well, she seems to know exactly what you're thinking . . .

In fact, after only a few seconds, Doris has already done a lot more for my sex drive than *Mr* Sullivan ever managed!

'She *was* very beautiful,' Mr Sullivan says, and takes a deep breath. Then he lets loose with the longest, most tremendous sigh I've ever encountered. 'But boy, did she make my life a living hell.'

On the bureau there are fake eyelashes, fake pearls, fake diamond brooches, fake rubies and sapphires. When I open a plastic-covered jewelry box it gives off a broken chiming sound, like the time Marvin backed over Tony's bike in the driveway. The jewelry box contains fading yellow food coupons clipped from newspapers and magazines.

'Doris came to Southern California to be a movie star,' Mr Sullivan tells me. 'She had seven brothers and four sisters, and all she wanted was attention. When she couldn't become a movie star, she married me and pre-tended to be crippled. I used to push her around all day in that big stainless steel wheelchair. To the park or the grocery store. Or out to the car for a long drive down the coast.'

Mr Sullivan is lying on his back on the bed, staring at the white ceiling. 'I loved every minute of it. Here I was, not much to look at, married to this beautiful woman in a wheelchair. It was terribly romantic. But then the years went by and Doris lost her looks. She got crabbier and crabbier the less attention people paid to her. She didn't allow me one decent night's sleep in twenty years. Always in the middle of the night I'd feel her nudging me with her pointy elbow. Warm milk she needed. Or ice-cream. Noises in the attic or mice in the walls.'

I pull on a fake cashmere robe from one of the bureau drawers. The fake cashmere is peeling like an old sun-stained vinyl rooftop on an automobile. I get up and go to the window. Outside the back yard is all lit up like this miniature putt-putt golf course.

'It's not like she lost the will to live or anything,' Mr Sullivan is saying. (I like Mr Sullivan when he gets like this – not so attentive to me personally, I mean.) 'But she grew determined not to let me enjoy my life so long as she was still living. She spent most of her time sitting up in bed waiting for me to come in the room. She'd look at my clothes. She'd look at my hair, my teeth, my eyes. I could see her expression going click, click, click. Did I pay the electricity? Did I tip the newspaper boy? Did I change the oil in the car, or have the brakes checked, or the windshield wipers? Did I remember to pick up my paycheck? How much was it and why not more? Eventually, you see, Doris exercised her will to live through my body. I wasn't a separate person anymore. I was someone who existed to remind Doris of how far she could still reach, and how much control she still possessed. It was like one of those, what do you call them? Symbiotic relationships. Like the parasite that cleans the shark's eyeballs? That was us. The parasite and the shark.'

What a depressing back yard, I think. It has been completely paved over with concrete, with a few long rectangles of gravel. There's a picnic table on the patio, but who cares? It's not the sort of place anybody would ever go for a picnic.

'So then she had a heart attack,' I say. I am watching my reflection in the window. I am only half there, divided right down the middle like the moon outside. 'Doris wore herself out hating you, even though you did everything you could for her. But then she had a heart attack and died.'

Mr Sullivan gives me that long terrible sigh again. Being with Mr Sullivan in his big empty house seems too intimate and clean, slightly wrong somehow. Mr Sullivan and I should either be a lot closer together or a lot farther apart.

'Well, sort of,' Mr Sullivan says, just before he confesses everything. 'That's *sort* of how it happened.'

Who ever would have guessed?

I insist on driving myself home, claiming that I need my 'own space' for a while, which actually is pretty true and not the phoney excuse it sounds like. The need for personal 'space' is an idea I'm getting more and more used to lately. I mean like space in the worldly sense and not just the space inside my own head.

The space inside my own head, meanwhile, is buzzing with possibilities. Husbands and wives all over America knocking one another off, as casually as mowing the lawn or sweeping the floor. But what do you read in the newspaper? Heart attacks, bad blood, shot by burglar, disappeared without forwarding address, too much cholesterol and not enough bran, suicide, accidental drowning, finger caught in wall-plug, fell down stairs, forgot to take medication. It's as if the surface of the world and the things happening underneath the surface never quite match – but then, why *should* they?

If everything happened like it was supposed to, that would make life pretty boring, wouldn't it?

Well?

Murdering your spouse for no other reason than you hate their guts. What other possible reason is there?

Trying to be serious for a moment, let's consider this idea from all possible angles. First off, there are two objections to the manslaughter-style-alleviation-of-marital-discomforts theory. One is legal and the other is moral. The legal one – who cares? Since when have legal objections done anybody any good except the damn lawyers? And the moral one, well, I'm not so presumptuous or egotistical to say I know what's moral and what's not. I mean, I never even went to college or anything.

So this is how I look at it. Life's short. None of us is going to be around for ever. So if you're unhappy with your spouse or your spouse is a dreadfully nasty and selfish person who doesn't deserve to live (and who knows better than you since you've been shacked up with them all these years?) then why not go ahead and bump them off? I mean, especially if nobody's going to miss them but you.

There should be some sort of age limit, though. I mean, so newly weds don't go bumping each other off over silly things like infidelity or mis-squeezing the toothpaste tube. Say, thirty years of really bad marriage. Then you've got the right to bump off your spouse if you want to. But before that you have to put up with them – no matter what. (Unless of course they are violent types who physically abuse you or the children. In that case you can bump them off whenever you want to, no problem.)

You can bump them off, that is, but only so long as you don't get caught.

When I get home I fix myself a *tiny* brandy. Just enough to keep the warm buzz going. It's almost four a.m. and I'm not tired at all. There's this nice glow of moonlight coming through the white curtains. A nice white haze. Each piece of furniture in the living room looks very content with its own inner essence. The place is as clean as I left it, since Marvin hasn't bothered me once since I riddled his dead body with the Remington.

I can't stop thinking how clever Mr Sullivan is.

When I finish my first brandy I pour myself just the *teensiest* second one and go downstairs to the basement where Marvin's old work bench is covered with dust and oily rags. I take down the long extension cord from the nail on the wall. Then I go upstairs to the kitchen and unplug the toaster and shake it over the sink to get rid of the crumbs.

Then I go upstairs and run some water in the bath.

While the water's running I plug one end of the extension cord into the wall and the other into the toaster.

'I took a trip on a train,' I sing, remembering my favorite singer, Dinah Washington. 'And I thought about you. I thought about you.' I'm watching the tub fill with clear bluish water. I feel so happy I just have to keep singing:

> And every stop that we made
> I thought about you, I thought about you.

Some days everything seems so simple. The brandy has given me a nice little jolt and I can't stop smiling. The toaster is humming in my hands like a newborn baby.

'Hey, Doris!' I shout at the empty tub. 'Your husband, Mr Sullivan, told me to give you *this*!'

Then I toss in the toaster.

And everything goes black.

18

When I wake up the next morning it's practically noon and I'm back in my own bed. The phone on my end table is ringing off the hook.

The first time I say hello nothing comes out.

'Is that you, Emma?'

Of course it's me. But at this point I'm afraid to look in the mirror to check. My mouth tastes like that stuff the kids used to get in the new carpets. Silly Putty.

(Have you ever tried scraping Silly Putty out of the carpets? It's absolutely impossible.)

'Listen, Emma,' he says. 'About last night.'

I sit up and reach for my radio alarm clock. The face of the clock is completely black, and at first I think maybe it has come unplugged. Then I remember.

Doris in the bathtub.

'Don't worry, Mr Sullivan,' I tell him very quickly. I'm trying the lamp switch, the wall switch, and of course nothing works. I'm saying, 'Because we're both mature adults—'

'I don't mean that,' he says suddenly. He's squeezing his voice into the telephone so nobody else can hear, which is especially ridiculous since Mr Sullivan lives alone. 'I mean the things I *told* you.'

'Oh,' I say, and wipe my nose with a Kleenex. I feel like it's time somebody buried *me* in the garden ASAP.

After a moment Mr Sullivan's silence on the line starts to make me nervous.

'I wouldn't worry about that either, Mr Sullivan,' I say. 'Your secret's safe with me.'

By the time I get downstairs in my blue robe and slippers the entire household is a holy mess, just like a bomb hit it or something, or a herd of stampeding cattle from what used to be my favorite TV show, *Rawhide*. There are over-turned chairs and dirty dishes everywhere and two empty bottles of brandy on the floor. The curtains are drawn open on all the windows, and even though the white sun is flashing in the back yard the inside of the house seems gray and dismal, as if the inside and the outside belong to two different dimensions. Outside, everything seems so sunny and beautiful it couldn't possibly be real. Inside everything seems thick with reality, and very depressing as a result. Dust motes are whirling everywhere and I smell something cheesy in the kitchen trash-bag.

After rummaging around in a drawer I finally find the packet of fuses. I also find tangles of string, plastic yellow corn-cob finger-grips, rusty bobby-pins, petrified crinkly tubes of airplane glue, a furry fragment of something which might once have been meat, a litter of baby dust-bunnies, old rumpled utility bills, yet another business card from Marvin's rotten lawyer, Mr Oswald Spengler (the most annoying man I've probably never met), and not to men-tion one of Thomas's old report cards. (C, C, C-, C, C, C-, C. *Pays too much attention to his friends, and not enough attention to his homework.* Tell me about it.)

When I take the fuse out to the back-yard fuse box what do I find but Marvin up and around again, digging a hole in the middle of the yard with the rusty shovel. He has cut away the scraggly brown turf into big shaggy pieces and stacked them beside the hole like chunks of mouldy carpet.

When I come outside Marvin stops for a minute and leans against the shovel. He is standing about knee high in a fresh brown trough of dirt. Except for one quick acciden-tal glance I refuse to look at him.

'For years I told you we should build a bomb shelter,' he tells me. 'But *you* wanted a garden.'

I go to the fusebox and pry it open with a screwdriver I keep on the outside window ledge for this very purpose. The fuses are all charred and smoky inside and hard to get a good grip on, especially since my fingernails aren't as strong as they used to be.

'If we had a bomb shelter like I orginally *intended*,' Marvin continues, 'we could just open the lid and drop them in. There wouldn't be all this messy digging around with shovels and whatnot.'

'I'm not listening,' I tell Marvin out loud. I have replaced three fuses and am having a little trouble unscrewing the fourth. 'You can babble on all you want, Marvin. But I've got better things to do than listen.'

I can feel the shape of Marvin over my shoulder, and from my quick earlier glimpse I can tell he has definitely seen better days. Parts of his face seem to be falling off, and there are big gaping holes in his clothes where I punctured him soundly with the Remington, or maybe it was the long steel spikes. Wormy things are dripping from his stomach and chest which might either be his insides or maybe just lawn slugs.

'You're a big smelly box of dog hair,' Marvin says cheerily. It seems to make him very happy to have some-body to yell at again. 'You're a squatting wooden pig-faced baboon. Why don't you go watch TV, Emma? That's about all you're good for.'

I refuse to let Marvin hurt my feelings anymore, and since I can't get the fourth fuse unscrewed I close the fuse box and march right back into the house.

'Guess who the new hole's for, Emma? I'll give you two guesses.'

But I shut the picture window without looking back. Then I pull shut the curtains.

All the lights in the living room are on but the light doesn't seem real somehow. Someone on the TV is saying, 'Look, Marshall. If you hadn't gotten me pregnant there wouldn't *be* a problem.'

I stand there in the living room a moment. I seem to have gotten totally out of breath.

Then, after another minute, Marvin starts up again.

Hish. Shuhh. *Hish*. Shuhh.

Then the shovel scraped against a rock or a piece of buried metal and stops again. It pauses a few more minutes. Then:

Hish. Shuhh. *Hish*. Shuhh.

Well, I tell myself, look on the bright side.

After more than forty years of marriage you've finally gotten that lazy pig to do a little gardening!

In the living room I discover that Marvin has opened all my mail, even the junk mail. The junk mail mainly consists of endless computerized letters from the Church of Immaculate Reason requesting more donations, along with their various slick magazines and newsletter-brochures. The magazine covers are illustrated with dragons and alien spaceships, and carry endorsements from various media celebrities and science fiction authors. 'A triumph of the rational mind!' declares Roger Enright, author of the *Winged Marauder* series. 'Taught me how to love again!' declares Annie Unruh, co-star of the so-called 'hit' TV sitcom, *The Pattersons* (though I've certainly never heard of it).

When I pick up the magazine it opens automatically to an article entitled 'Self-Love Through Self-Rule: Back in the Saddle Again!'

'The Masters of Destruction take many forms in our multi-faceted universe,' this article proclaims. 'Sometimes they even take the form of our very own selves! Have *you* been clarified lately?'

The stacks of computerized junk mail are almost all addressed to Marvin O'Hallahan, or to Mr and Mrs Marvin O'Hallahan, or to the entire O'Hallahan family. But one letter is addressed just to Dear Emma, and I can't help pulling it from the stack and giving it a good once over.

Dear Emma

I am deeply aggrieved to hear of your recent loss. And since I know how frustrating it is to receive nothing more than the usual 'form-letter' condolences, I have taken a little time out from my busy schedule to address your situation personally.

Marvin was definitely a fine, generous member of the Church, and will be sorely missed from our Earth-bound continuum.

But, however lonely you may feel, I want you to know that we here at the Church are deeply concerned with your recovery from mortal-grief. Remember that shortly before this unfortunate demise, your husband Marvin was clarified (through our convenient direct-mail program) of all improper resident-beings and pre-birth stereotypes – and all this for a paltry contribution of *less* than one hundred dollars per month! Since he has been successfully clarified, death does not mark the end of his existence, but rather liberates him to travel through the universe as a freedom-loving Remetron, a form of existence one step upwards in the universal process of spiritual advancement.

Doesn't that sound nice?

I've read your request that we stop sending you our literature. I have, however, taken a personal interest in your spiritual growth and well-being.

Don't say I didn't warn you!

Yours affectionately,
Colonel Robert Robertson

P.S.   Very shortly you will be receiving an amazing offer from my personal attorney, Mr Oswald Spengler. Are you ready to take control of your own life and unleash the untapped potential of your trans-human brain? Then please listen carefully to Mr Spengler's generous proposal.

Oh great, I think. Just what I need. Personal-growth attention. And as if that's not enough – more lawyers!

I sit down on the stuffed chair, which is scratchy with crumpled envelopes and Pringles' bits. My head hurts like crazy and my legs are throbbing even worse than usual. What have I done to deserve all this?

Oh, maybe a few things, I guess.

At this point, I see Marvin's shape looming against the curtains of the picture window. His shadow is heavy and dark like really bad weather. When he pounds on the glass the entire window frame chatters.

'I'm not a monster!' Marvin shouts. (So loud the entire neighborhood can't help hearing.) 'I'm a human being with feelings and integrity!'

'Fooled me, Marvin,' I say.

'You think *I'm* evil?' he shouts. 'Well, what about *you*? Do you have any idea what I went thought living with a human-shaped hunk of drooling mental retardation such as yourself? Other men had wives who *appreciated* or even *loved* them, for Christ's sake. But *I* worked hard all day building a home for you and our children and what thanks did I get? I'll tell you what thanks I got. I got to sit around day after day listening to some addle-pated, big-butted moron droning on about cheesecake and roast beef and how fresh the vegetables looked at Von's. What a nice day today! Guess how much I saved on beets! Isn't the mailman a really *nice person*! Mindless droning incomprehensible blather, day after endless day of it, week after insurmountable week! And then, of course, the eternal cringing and whining! Oh yes, honey, Oh, right away, sweetheart, Oh of course, dear. And all the time she's sweet-talking me I *know* all she can think about is loading up my best shotgun and blowing my cranial tissue all over the new wallpaper! You don't think it surprised me, do you, Emma? Hell, no! In fact, I actually *welcomed* it! I was looking *forward* to a premature eternity living alone in the garden – that's how miserable *I* was! But does it turn out that way? I mean, even after being *murdered* by my own lawfully wedded wife do you think I find one *minute* of peace and quiet out here? Oh no, Emma! *That* would've been too *fair*!'

I have clamped my hands over my ears and begun humming to myself. La-de-da-da, I hum. La-de-da-da-da-*daaaah*. But then I hear the second voice anyway, as clearly as if it's coming from my own mouth.

'Emma? Is that you?'

I can feel the shape of her emerging from the garden before I look up. Even her shadow against the curtain is unmistakable, like the way she always knocked at my door or rung my buzzer.

'Do you know your husband is driving me completely crazy?'

Mrs Stansfield is trying to see through the glare by holding her two hands against the outer glass.

'You want to know how much sense of communal responsibility he possesses? Absolutely zero, Emma. Zero – abso*lutely*. And you want to know what solution he proposes for every political problem in our country today – from freedom of choice through this whole Yugoslavia mess? Blowing somebody's brains out with a gun. As if that was ever a meaningful answer to *anything*.'

'Maybe sometimes it's an answer,' I whisper to myself. 'Sometimes you don't have any choice.'

I take my hands off my ears since it isn't doing any good anyway. Upstairs the radio alarm clock has started buzzing.

'He's unbearable, Emma,' Mrs Stansfield cries, just to make me feel guilty. 'And now you've locked me out here with him *forever*.'

'I'm sorry,' I say. I know it's a mistake to encourage them but I say it anyway. 'I really am, Mrs Stansfield. I wasn't in my right mind or something. When I shot Marvin, I definitely *was* in my right mind, but when I shot you, well. I was suffering seriously paranoid delusions. I think it may have been on account of my lousy diet and poor body management. Or maybe I really *am* going a little senile, just like Marvin keeps saying.'

'A *little* senile?' Marvin shouts. 'Emma – you started out

a *little* senile! What you've got now is called galloping dementia!'

Always Mr Critical, I think. If he ever had anything nice to say he'd probably choke on it.

'I don't know who made you such a big brain expert, Marvin,' I tell him.

Mrs Stansfield says, 'Now don't you two start.'

'It doesn't take a brain surgeon to tell you've gone totally wacko, Emma. Some seventy-year-old moronic female starts shooting people and burying them in the garden – we don't exactly need a trained psychotherapist to tell us whether she's mentally stable or not.'

Finally I speak up. It's pretty obvious that if *anybody* is going to stick up for my side of things, it'll have to be me.

'You make it sound as if I've been behaving irrationally, Marvin,' I tell him. 'You make it sound as if I've been shooting people at random without any good reason whatsoever, but that's where you're wrong. Maybe my reasons aren't entirely correct, and perhaps I've gone overboard a little, but that doesn't mean I haven't thought things through. And just so you don't forget, Mr Know-it-All – I'm not seventy. I'm only sixty-nine.'

But Marvin, as per usual, doesn't stop to listen. He just keeps yelling: 'It's getting awfully *crowded* out here, Emma!'

'Which reminds me,' Mrs Stansfield butts in. 'Who's buried in the third grave, Emma? I need to know.'

'Who do you *think's* buried in the third grave, you old coot?' Marvin's silhouette is shaking his shovel around for emphasis.

'I don't know,' I tell her. 'I'm afraid I honestly don't know.'

'Let's take a guess,' Marvin says. 'Let me see . . . Could it be someone intimately related to us, perchance?'

'It's *not* one of our grandchildren,' I say quickly, before I lose Mrs Stansfield's respect completely.

But Mrs Stansfield is already saying, 'Oh, Emma . . .'

'He's just making that up,' I tell her. I stand up and go to the window. I can feel her weight and heat coming through the curtains at me. 'And even if it *is* my grandchild, it's not necessarily my fault. I wasn't in my right frame of mind for a few days there. But starting this morning I'm going to take better care of myself – both physically *and* mentally. And this time I mean it. I'm *really* laying off that crazy brandy.'

'Oh Emma,' Mrs Stansfield says again. And again and again and again.

I really wish she'd stop staying that.

19

By the time Mr Sullivan drops by in the afternoon I am completely snockered. I have finished off the brandy, what's left of the wine, two dusty cans of Marvin's old Stout Malt Liquor, and something in a glass jar which might have been home-made liqueur someone gave us for Christmas. I've eaten all the fish sticks and the Chips Ahoy cookies. There are dirty dishes everywhere, some of them mine and some of them Marvin's. And just to make this entire afternoon a monument to self-indulgence, I'm watching my favorite soap opera, *Loving to Share*, on the living-room TV.

I'm still wearing my slippers and robe and I've got my feet propped up on the antique coffee table.

'You have to forget the past,' Josh Greenport is telling his former lover, Trish Van Doren. 'The past is over. What we had is no longer.'

When the doorbell rings I shout, 'Come in!' But I don't want to get up because I still have a little brandy left in my glass. Whenever I think about how sad Josh and Trish have been since their 'break-up' I get so weepy!

'Emma!' Mr Sullivan shouts from the front porch. 'Are you in there?'

'Come in!' I yell. But then I'm leaning into the TV to hear better, because now it's Trish's turn to speak.

'But the past is always with us, Josh. We can't live with it, but we can't live without it.'

How true. I'm already weeping uncontrollably.

'Emma?' Mr Sullivan shouts, and rings the doorbell a few more times.

'Come in!' I shout.

'No matter how hard we try to bury the past,' Josh says, 'we can't ever escape it.' Josh is standing behind Trish with his arms wrapped protectively around her. They have both turned their good sides to the camera. Trish is so lovely when she's sad!

'I know,' Trish says. 'It's like Marvin, my husband whom I buried in the garden last month. He won't leave me alone. He's digging a big hole in the garden and is threatening to give me a little bit back of what I gave him. In addition, we fight *constantly*. It's like we're still married.'

'Ex*act*ly,' I tell Trish sympathetically. I salute her with my glass and spill a little of my precious brandy, which I lick from the sides of my glass and the tips of my fingers. 'The bastard just won't stay down!'

I look at the back yard, from which I have drawn open the curtains. It's still sunny outside, and like me the birds are too hot to feel chirpy.

Then I see him, coming around the side of the house. He has changed his clothes. He's wearing a crisp white short-sleeve shirt, gray slacks and brown Hush Puppies.

'Lousy bastard,' I say, and put down my glass.

I'm looking around for any handy weaponry that might be available when he comes in through the open picture window.

'Well, honey,' Josh says supportively, 'have you ever tried firing a few rounds into his dead body with an HK-P7? That might teach him a thing or two.'

'Hello, Emma.' Mr Sullivan is standing in the picture window. He looks at me and the messy living room. Then he looks over his shoulder at the garden.

Finally, he turns to me and says, 'That's some hole you've dug in the garden, Emma.'

'Hush, Mr Sullivan,' I tell him. I try to reach for the TV's volume control but I misjudge how far away it is so I fall straight back into my chair.

'I've tried that,' Trish tells Josh. 'But oh, I don't know. *Nothing* seems to work anymore.' She sounds like one of those commercial housewives who's never heard of Extra-Strength Something-or-other.

Weeping, Trish turns her chin into her shoulder. (But of course her face doesn't get all swollen and snotty like mine does. Trish is beautiful even when she's suffering!)

Mr Sullivan sniffs in the direction of my ceiling. 'What's that buzzing noise, Emma? Is that a radio alarm?'

'Oh, poor Trish!' The tears are pouring down my face and splashing into my nearly empty glass. 'She tries so *hard* to be good!'

'I think somebody's had a little too much to drink.' Then I feel Mr Sullivan's hand on my shoulder. Then I see his other hand taking away my glass.

On the TV Trish is saying, 'Next time, maybe I'll douse the yard with gasoline and set the whole place on fire. Maybe *that'll* teach the bastard to stay put.'

I seem to sleep forever, but when I wake up again the radio alarm says it's only five-thirty. Outside my window it's very sunny and bright in the garden, as per usual.

Good morning, I tell my head. How are you feeling today?

And my head says right back: Boom boom boom boom boom.

Ow ow ow, I say.

Mr Sullivan is sleeping like a little angel, so saint-like and peaceful. He was very sweet to me last night. He kept handing me tall glasses of fizzy mineral water and saying, 'Here. Swallow a few glasses of this stuff. And a few more of these aspirin, too.'

After I pee I go into my office and switch on the light but they don't go on.

'Uh oh,' I remember. 'Still a bad fuse in the fuse box.'

I go downstairs to fix myself a pot of coffee and find that Mr Sullivan has cleaned everything. The dishes, the tables, the countertops, the floors. He has taken the big overflowing trash bags out to the garage. I think he's even gone over the living-room carpet with the carpet sweeper.

What a nice guy.

The back yard looks very peaceful and very terrible at the same time. I feel I could walk out into the peaceful sunlight and never come back.

The morning dew is shining everywhere, even on the mound of dirt next to Marvin's new hole in the yard. Everything smells fresh, and the old burial-mounds are starting to turn the same color as the rest of the yard. Time passes, as they say. Turn turn turn again.

Suddenly, standing there in the picture window, I realize I am not alone. There is somebody else out there.

Then I look up and see him. A big yellow cat on the fence, and he's looking straight at me.

I hiss.

'Get out of my yard,' I tell the cat. 'And leave those sweet birds alone.'

I take my coffee back upstairs, open my notebook and catch up on current events. I don't know where to start sometimes since, if nothing else, my life has become extremely event-filled lately. The funniest thing you learn from keeping a notebook is: you think at first you haven't got anything to say. But after a while you're always running out of time because there's too much to say.

Oh, well.

Meanwhile I'm looking through the drawers for an ink eraser when I come across one of Marvin's old 'philosophical projects'. This particular project is the one he was working on before his sudden and unfortunate demise at the hands of yours truly. It is entitled, much like my list on the bulletin board, What's Wrong with America (as if Marvin is the big expert on this, of course).

I open to the first page and it begins thusly:

The world is an illusion created by a race of sentient beings far more powerfully intelligent than most mere humans can possibly imagine!

Most mere humans, of course, with the definite exception of *me*!

For example. If *I* were running things, I'd force this screwy nation to shape up PDQ (pretty damn quick).

First, I'd build bigger prisons, just so the coloreds and Latins would know I meant business. Then I'd put all the homosexuals in mental detention centers where they would be indoctrinated into the proper use of their bodies, which is divine heterosexuality of course. Then I'd offer everybody big bucks in exchange for having themselves neutered, thus to decrease the world's surplus population problem. Once I'd tackled all such problems of morality and crime, I'd move on to global economics.

Watch out, world. Here I come.

Globally I would enforce strict price controls on all food and manufacturing products. If a country didn't want to listen, well, first we'd try reasoning with them. Then, if they didn't listen to reason, we'd blow them up. The world's in too big a mess to waste time arguing. Thus: inflation would be solved. Along with every tin-pot dictator who didn't listen to good old American know-how and common sense!

The tin-pot dictators who *did* listen to reason, however, would do pretty well under this new system of mine. And since their countries are filled with nothing but communistical trouble-makers, jigaboos and diaper-heads, then such tin-pot dictators are a necessary evil we need to help keep the Mutant Hordes under control.

So now morality, crime and economics are solved. 'But how about education?' you ask.

We give kids a no-nonsense high school education in basic skills and services. Like fixing cars, building houses, doing electrical work, emptying trash cans, you name it. Then we dispense with all the liberal arts bullshit, along with their terminally wacky PC-conscious instructors. This means no more tax dollars teaching people to fingerpaint, write poetry, or memorize the lies in history books and newspapers. It also means less time for lazy kids to sit around thinking up ways to piss off their elders, who, of course, know a lot more than they do.

There, so the education problem's solved. Pretty easy, huh?

Now since it's perfectly simple to solve our country's

various problems, why hasn't anybody solved them up to now? Or why hasn't the nation drafted *me* to solve them, since my ideas are so obviously correct. Give up? Okay, I'll tell you.

Because, to get back to my earlier point, the world is an illusion, that's why.

If the world were real, we could take care of all these simple problems simply by being realistic.

But you can't be realistic if the world's an illusion. Get it?

In other words, the trick is to endure the world's horseshit while keeping your mind straight, and not succumbing to the fascist fake-intelligentsia/thought-police who secretly rule our nation. You must remain totally reasonable all the time, even while pseudo-liberals like Dan Rather or Bruce Morton are telling you otherwise.

Then, when you die, you transcend this illusion and find your way onto the next plane of existence.

Which is, of course, the subject of my next chapter.

This is about all I can take of Marvin's so-called 'philosophical project', so I close his notebook and toss it in the trash.

'The next plane of existence, Marvin,' I say out loud, just in case he's listening, 'is a big hole I dug for you in our back yard. What do you think of *that*, Mr Know-It-All?'

I look over my shoulder. Then I look over my other shoulder.

All the lights in the office are still out. I can hear Mr Sullivan snoring peacefully next door in the master bedroom.

Before I finish work for the morning I take down *my* list entitled What's Wrong with America. I only have two more spaces left to fill in, but already I've figured out one of them.

9. Not enough men like Mr Sullivan in the world (even if he did kill his wife).

Mr Sullivan is still slumbering away like a baby when I go down to the garage and warm up the Oldsmobile. It's another beautiful day in Southern Cal, the radio is saying. Eat your heart out, New England.

I drive to the Arco station, which is just off the highway

at the edge of Dynamo Valley, and ask the boy there to fill it up with Ethel, which is not so easy to find anymore since everybody uses Unleaded.

Then I hand him the car keys to the trunk.

'And would you mind filling up those two empty gas cans I have back there?' I ask. 'My husband needs them for his power mower.'

I drop by the local Stop-and-Shop near the beach to pick up a few choice treats for Mr Sullivan. Cinnamon Rolls and Taster's Choice Café Mocha.

When I come into the front door with my small bag of groceries and two large red cans of Premium gasoline, Mr Sullivan shouts down at me from upstairs.

'Emma?'

'That's my name,' I tell him. 'Don't wear it out.'

'Someone rang the bell while you were gone!'

'Thank you, Mr Sullivan.'

It's still only eight a.m., so I figure it must be Marvin trying to ruin Mr Sullivan's beauty sleep. The thought of Marvin trying to ruin Mr Sullivan's beauty sleep makes me really mad.

That does it. If I haven't made up my mind already, I sure have now.

'Funny joke, Marvin,' I say. Then I take the gasoline cans out to the back porch and the grocery bag into the kitchen.

I open the cinnamon rolls and place a thick pat of butter on each one. Then I turn on the oven and put the cinnamon rolls on the cookie sheet.

'Guess what I'm fixing *you* for breakfast?' I shout upstairs.

'Eggs benedict!' Mr Sullivan shouts back.

'No way, Mr Sullivan! Something *much* better!'

The world is a very ironical place, I am thinking as I go out to the back porch. Take, for example my deceased husband Marvin and my current boyfriend, Mr Sullivan. Marvin is the sort of man who thinks he knows everything, but in reality he doesn't know anything. He considers himself some big expert on divine heterosexuality, for example, but boy is he lousy in the sack. He's a presumed master of global economics, but basically no more than a big ripoff artist who screwed people out of their mortgage arrangements whenever possible. He recognizes all the problems with our country but none of his own. Marvin for President – ha!

And then, on the other hand, there's Mr Sullivan, who admits his worse mistakes in life (though provoking Doris's tragic heart-attack wasn't a mistake at all, but probably totally justified, if you ask me) and yet he has no wish to be in control of anything or anybody. Good for you, Mr Sullivan. It takes courage for a man not to have big ambitions in this overly materialistic world of ours.

There are two types of people in the world, I decide. Those who think they should run the world, and of course they are all totally insane. Then there are the perfectly sane people who just want to be left alone to enjoy themselves the best they can. This means the world is doomed to be run only by people who are totally nuts, while the people who *should* be running things are considered nebishes or retards. I should probably name this theory of mine Emma's Law or something. What a world.

I am thinking Emma's Law obviously belongs at number ten on my What's Wrong with America list, but by this time I am too busy to go upstairs and write it down, since now I am splashing Premium grade gasoline all over the back yard. I am splashing it over the wooden porch, the rose bushes, and even around the sides of the fences. I am splashing it especially over Marvin's grave, and in the hole he's been digging in the grass, presumably because he thinks he's going to put me in it.

Then, suddenly, I remember.

I forgot to boil water for Mr Sullivan's Café Mocha!

When I go into the kitchen Mr Sullivan shouts down, 'Do you need any help in the kitchen, Emma?'

He's so sweet.

No, I tell him. Everything's under control.

I fill the kettle and put it on the stove. Then I go out to the back yard with a box of Blue Point matches from the fireplace.

Everything is perfectly silent out here all of a sudden. No Marvin, no Mrs Stansfield. Nobody digging big holes in the ground with a rusty shovel. No birds and no big yellow cat on the fence.

Perhaps Marvin thinks if he keeps very quiet I won't fry him to bits.

Sorry, Marvin.

Looking into the empty hole Marvin has been digging greets me with a funny sensation. Would it really be so terrible to be buried in the ground? It would mean no more decision-making. No more worries. No more bills to pay. No more terrible hay-fever every spring. Just the warm darkness. Forever and ever.

When I go back into the kitchen the teapot is hissing, so I turn the flame down to Lo. Then I take the Colt from the kitchen drawer and go back out to the yard, where, boy, does the place sure smell of gasoline!

'Now we're even, Marvin,' I tell him. I show my gun around. 'Tit for tat.'

Marvin has yet to make an appearance, though. I think he's even more scared than I am.

Holding the gun carefully in my left hand I splash more gasoline around until there are a few shimmery puddles in the dry grass. Then I pull up the green lawn chair to sit down. (I can't crouch on account of my legs.)

'Good riddance,' I say out loud, which is about as dramatic a line as I can manage. I lean forward over the big hole in the yard.

Then, holding the gun to my head with my left hand, I strike the handy Blue Point match against the rusty aluminum frame of my lawn chair.

The match hisses and flares. I touch it to one of the little puddles of gasoline.

All in one moment I shut my eyes and squeeze my finger on the trigger. I can't help thinking: This is one part of my life I can't write down for posterity.

And then it happens.

Nothing.

Absolutely nothing happens.

The gun turns soft and clayey in my hand and I realize: dumb Emma. I forgot to turn off the safety switch.

When I open my eyes again, I see a small flickering yellow flame in the puddle of gasoline. The flame shrinks away, charring the grass, and extinguishes. It leaves a black circle on the grass, like those charcoal snakes I used to buy the kids for Fourth of July.

Quickly I lean over and strike another match just as I hear the front doorbell starting to buzz.

Oh, fiddlesticks.

'I'm coming!' I shout.

But when I touch the next match to the grass, nothing happens. The little puddles of gasoline have completely evaporated.

How totally undramatic!

Maybe I'll get to write this foolish escapade of your nana's down in my diary, after all.

20

The doorbell's still buzzing when I come back inside and Mr Sullivan's shouting:

'Have you got that, Emma? Emma?'

Needless to say, I am feeling pretty dispirited by the time I reach the door. If Marvin is up to any of his old tricks, I'm afraid I'm not going to be very patient with him this morning. I'm wondering how many cans of gasoline it will take to turn the back yard into a properly raging inferno. Possibly thousands.

Then I look through the spyglass in my door and see this weird, elongated face with a crewcut on top.

The doorbell starts buzzing again.

'Emma!' Mr Sullivan shouts.

'Hold your horses, everybody,' I say. Then I place the Colt in the pocket of my dress and open the door.

He isn't much taller than I am, and carrying a small gray canvas backpack over his shoulder. He's wearing a lime-green T-shirt and blue jeans and is far more handsome than I'd have expected from somebody with his genetic background.

'Like hey, Nana,' he tells me. 'How you doing. It's *me*.'

I can hardly believe my eyes.

Then he squints and looks over my shoulder at the living room. He wiggles his nose and scowls, as if he just swallowed something disgusting.

He says, 'Like, Nana. What's that burning I smell?'

Burning?
Oh no. Could it possibly . . .
And right away I know it is.
Mr Sullivan's cinnamon rolls!

21

It starts raining that morning and doesn't let up all day.

'There's nothing wrong with a desire for transcendence,' Teddy tells us at breakfast, 'especially if you're American. Transcendence is what made this country great in the first place, because it's the dream of better places to go than anybody's ever been before. Wider horizons, bigger shopping malls, more sex, fatter steaks, warmer beaches, better jobs and higher pay. What Americans want is what they haven't already got. And that's why they came here, Nana. To California. To get everything they never got all over again. We're the trailblazers of the trailblazers, sort of like immigrant immigrants but with *lots* more baggage. California is America squared. It's the place you go to find more America than you ever thought possible. Someday, Nana, like the *next* race of Californians? We're going to hurl ourselves into the sea just like lemmings. Do you think that's why *lemmings* do it, Nana? Because they're smart enough to want more but not smart enough to know when it's been all used up?'

Mr Sullivan and I are sitting at the kitchen table watching Teddy eat his eggs. Scrambled eggs with cheese. I'm wearing my robe, Mr Sullivan's wearing Marvin's.

'I guess I'm what you'd have to call the ultimate Californian,' Teddy tells us, 'being as I've probably expanded my transcendental awareness so far it's ridiculous. My mom – or who you probably still think of as *your* daughter, Nana –

is a deeply industrious individual, at least so far as matters of personal awareness go. She has trouble keeping a job or a boyfriend for long, but in her constant search for spiritual inner peace and fulfillment she's taken me places most kids my age would never *dream* of going. I've broken bread with the Rajneesh, Nana. I've heightened my consciousness with TM, peyote, psilocybin, bad acid, theosophy, Marx, non-penetrative sex, heroin, EST, and even a few Boy Scout field trips. I've experimented with the pleasures of every conceivable type of heterosexual and homosexual encounter, and ultimately I've learned that I'm not interested in any sexual contact whatsoever – at least not if it involves another human being. *Homo sapiens*, Nana. Hairless bipeds with opposable thumbs – frankly, I guess they just make me nervous. Which means that now I tend to masturbate a lot and watch too much cable TV. I've been through group therapy, prep school, the 4-H Club, AA, and the state's recently updated Methadone program. And you want to know something, Nana? I really *have* learned a lot about myself. I've gone so far inside myself I've come right back out the other side. I've assimilated. I've grown. I've accepted my limitations as a material entity. This is *me*, Nana, and I'm *glad*.'

Teddy shows us a small fuzzy hole in his lime-green T-shirt, just so we know what his material entity looks like.

'And now I don't want to be anybody else,' he tells us. 'At least not until my next spiritual rebirth, when I hope to be reincarnated as either a fun-loving porpoise or an African Green parrot. Did you know that African parrots live for hundreds of years, Nana? That's because they're the eyes and ears of God.'

Mr Sullivan and I are finished with our coffee. Outside the wind is throwing leaves against the windows and stirring twigs in the yard. Teddy is all long limbs, knobbly joints and twitchy adam's apple. Very skinny, very pale, but even a little handsome once you get used to him.

Mr Sullivan is leaning his elbows on the table, pretending to sip coffee from his empty cup. He glances secretly over the rim of his cup at Teddy, then at me, then back at Teddy again. Mr Sullivan looks like a soldier hiding in a trench, watching enemy tanks rumble back and forth.

I look at Teddy. Teddy looks at me.

Then Teddy looks at the robe I'm wearing. He looks at Mr Sullivan.

'Mr Sullivan is staying with me for a few days while your grandpa's away,' I tell him. 'I get a little scared when I'm on my own.'

Teddy continues smiling. He raises his hands over his head as if he's being held up by friendly bank-robbers.

'Hey, Nana – you're a grown woman, right? You just keep on doing what you got to do.'

After Mr Sullivan goes home and Teddy starts taking his bath upstairs, I open the curtains on the picture window and sit with my glass of brandy looking at the yard. The wind is still knocking bushes around and the rain starts up again, washing away mounds of dirt near the hole where Marvin's been digging. I can hear the rushing water in the creek, where tall trees are swinging back and forth, and I'm wondering why is everybody so quiet? Where's Marvin? Where's Mrs Stansfield? And where, oh where, is Emma O'Hallahan? Emma, who surprises me more and more every day.

This is me, I whisper. This is me in here.

I take my brandy upstairs and go from one sound of water to another. Teddy running the bath and singing to himself in a high, distracted voice. Water hissing through overhead pipes, or gurgling in rain gutters outside, or dripping from trees and rooftops. As if there's perfect order in the universe, and one simple, beautiful idea running through everything.

Water.

Water making sense of everything.

Teddy has unpacked his little knapsack on the sofa in the gun room, which is where I told him he could stay and which used to be Thomas's room. Teddy's knapsack contains another lime-green T-shirt, a well-worn Guatemalan wool sweater, a package of 'Extra Safe' condoms, a tooth-brush, a handy pump-dispenser of New Tartar Control Formula Crest, and a pair of loose khaki pajama bottoms.

Good for you, Teddy. Travel light: that's my motto. (And I *would* have traveled light, too. If I'd ever gotten around to doing any traveling, that is.)

Finally I go into my office and shut the door. I hear water against the windows, circulating through the walls and ceiling. I finish my last glass of brandy of the day (I *promise*) and open my diary. Then, knowing I shouldn't, I go ahead and do for the second time what I once promised myself I'd *never* do *ever*.

So much for promises.

After a couple hours reading through this diary of my inner life and thoughts, I learn some interesting things about myself. First off, I hear what my own voice sounds like, which surprises me that I even have one, really. I never knew a voice was something you could put down in a notebook and save for future generations. But actually this diary contains the way Emma O'Hallahan really spoke and sounded in her life (however confused or even ditzy she may have been at times) which includes her total inner-being and personality essence, preserved like a biological specimen in a formaldehyde jar.

Maybe by writing myself down like this I will live for ever. Maybe my autobiography will even be published – posthumously, of course, since I'd personally find it too embarrassing being interviewed, and receiving literary prizes and so forth (not that I'd mind being *nominated* or anything). If, by chance, this volume of my thoughts and ambitions *does* get published, then I hereby decree that its total profits should go to you kids and grandkids (and maybe even *great* grandkids!) since maybe it will help you go to college and technical schools, etc. Who knows, maybe after I'm dead and buried (though I want to be cremated first) I will finally accomplish all the travelling I always dreamed of doing, since my widely reprinted autobio-graphy could very well be translated into many foreign languages, or taken along as 'light reading' on holiday cruises by tourists both American and foreign.

Boy, will I be happy. I'll be dead, but I'll also be really happy.

Meanwhile, reading through my record of the last few weeks it doesn't take a psychological genius or anything to notice that I'm rapidly losing grasp of Reality (not that I ever had a very firm grasp of Reality to begin with). Reality is a place which never had much to offer me, except more work to do, and more negative-sounding remarks about my intelligence, looks, personality and so forth. Sometimes Reality would sneak up behind me and go *bump!*, usually when I least expected it, like a gigantic face peering into my aquarium. Even when I thought I was far away from Reality, Reality was never very far away from me.

Until lately, that is.

For instance. Now that I've read through my diaries and recollections, I've started wondering how many of these events really happened, and how many of them are just made up. When I say made up, I mean made up in one of two ways: 1. Made up deliberately by my crazy imagination in order to 'spice up' my autobiography, or 2. Made up by my subconscious mind, which is trying to tell me things about my lousy childhood, and who knows what other horrible deeds and thoughts I've kept repressed over the years?

What with my terribly deteriorating memory lately, I don't even remember some of the simplest events that occurred in the last few days or so, such as my conversation with Officer Rodrigues, or my weirdly concerned letter from Colonel Robert Robertson, or how my conversation with Mr Spengler about the will turned out.

You can see my predicament.

Another for instance. If your dead grandpa's ghost has really been visiting me so often, then where is he now? Did he actually dig the hole in the garden for me? Or is he planning some other brand of mischief entirely, such as murdering Mr Sullivan (out of jealousy), or Teddy (your grandpa never liked Teddy's mother, Cassie), or perhaps even Officer Rodrigues (mainly because of his Latin extraction, though I'm sure your grandpa could come up with a million good reasons for hating someone as sweet as Officer Rodrigues).

Or did *I* dig the latest hole in the yard, just like I dug the other holes for Marvin, Mrs Stansfield, and the mysterious occupant of Grave Number 3?

Or do any of the holes actually exist?

(Do I?)

This is obviously where things start getting pretty scary.

Just imagine it – me, Emma O'Hallahan, not really existing in Reality unless I keep writing *constantly*! And if I stop writing for a moment? Poof, I vanish and never appear in this time-space dimension ever again! And what if I'm not writing anything at all, but am actually locked away in a nuthouse somewhere, doped up with drugs to keep me from hurting myself, and this whole diary is just something I've dreamed up to while away the time?

These are scary ideas in one way. But in another way, they are weirdly comforting ideas, too. Just imagine being able to do such powerful things with your life, armed with nothing more spectacular than a pencil and a loose-leaf notebook! Suddenly I am not foolish tiresome old Emma anymore. Suddenly I am master of time, space and dimension. I am the Master Creator of my own Environmental Capacity Scenario, just like the Supreme Being described by Colonel Robert Robertson in his nutty science fiction theories.

And what if I'm simply making things up? In fact, what if I'm sitting here right now inventing a whole lot of crazy goings on that never really happened? Maybe I'm even making up my house in Dynamo Valley, and my study, and my grandson Teddy. Maybe I'm actually in Bermuda surrounded by sexy young boys, spending Marvin's savings account like it's going out of style.

Who's to know otherwise?

Okay, so let's say I *am* master of time, space, dimension, etc. Maybe my life would go a little like this:

Here I am sitting in my office, writing my memoirs, when your dead grandpa comes marching into the room, eating a banana and acting like he owns the place.

I say to him:
    Hello, Marvin.
And he says right back:
    Hello, Emma.

ME

Well, Marvin, what a puzzle, huh? Where have you been for the last few days, and do you really exist at all? These are two very important questions which concern me very deeply right now.

YOUR GRANDPA

Oh Emma, you withering blob of putrescent donkey-puss. Why don't you wake up and smell the coffee? You're suffering from senile dementia, for crying out loud. This dementia is complicated by severe abuse of alcohol and Valium, along with a life-long disregard for Reality-As-We-Know-It. Face it, old girl. You're becoming a danger to everybody – even to the people you love.

ME

Not to my grandson, Marvin. Not to Mr Sullivan.

YOUR GRANDPA

I'm afraid so, leech-brain. Even to your beloved sex-toy, Mr Sullivan. Even to your beloved grandkids – Teddy, Wanda, Thomas Jr., and even What's-her-name. The little baby of Thomas's, you know.

ME
(refusing to be pushed around)

You tried telling me that once before, Marvin – remember?
You tried to tell me I'd buried my own grandson in the back
yard. Even though I knew better all along.

Your Grandpa tosses his half-eaten banana on the end-
table. Then he looks at me as if *I'm* the one who's crazy!

YOUR GRANDPA

I never told you anything of the sort, Emma. That was just
another of your crazy delusions. Hell, *I* don't even exist
right this minute, since I'm really just another creative
fabrication in your idiotic diary. And excuse me for butting
in, Emma, but if you're expecting this lump of knotty worm-
feces to be translated into several foreign languages, well.
Think again, old girl.

Suddenly I am so angry I can't see straight. Pure red anger
blazing through my heart and face. Just *remembering* the
sorts of horrible things your grandpa used to tell me – it's
like he really *is* still alive, replaying himself over and over
again in my mind whether I want him to or not. It's
enough to make me wish for us both to be reincarnated –
just so I could shoot that miserable bastard over and over
again. And again and again and again and again.

YOUR GRANDPA
(his usual wise-ass self)

Uh-oh, Emma. I think we're talking major psychotic episode
coming on. I'll warn you just this once. Stay *away* from my
gun collection.

ME

I'll stay away from your gun collection, Marvin. I'll stay away from *your* gun collection. I'll stay away from *your* gun collection, Marvin. I'll stay away from *your* gun collection.

At this point, while I am scribbling frantically to keep up with my overly imaginative encounter with Marvin, the door opens and Teddy pokes his wet head into the room.

TEDDY

Hey, Nana. I thought I heard you in here.

ME

Hi, Teddy. It's just me talking to myself while I write things in my diary—

Teddy looks around but doesn't see his grandpa, which is, of course, because his grandpa is nothing more than a product of my own personal creative juices. Teddy shrugs.

TEDDY

Cool, Nana. Whatever.

When Teddy closes the door again your grandpa can't wait to say something nasty.

YOUR GRANDPA

Bit swish, isn't he?

Everything is terribly noisy in my head, like static on a radio turned up loud. It's terribly confusing, but it's also totally real – even if it *is* made up. After all – this is *my* imaginative world, isn't it?

ME
(in complete emotional control of myself and definitely not sounding as if I'm having a psychotic episode)

How would you know, Marvin? How would you know? How would *you* know? How would you know *anything*!

22

First thing next morning I try the combination hardware store and lumberyard. (This is, incidentally, the same place I bought the steel poles for your grandpa's recently acquired acupuncture lesson.)

The manager is a nice blond man named Ray who asks me, 'You're talking about what sort of tree stump, Emma?'

I give it a good double-think. Let me see. My back yard is about twenty yards by fifteen yards. Then there are the fences, the concrete walkway and the wooden porch.

'A pretty big tree stump,' I tell Ray. 'Pretty big and deep.'

'Well,' Ray says. He is stroking his chin and looking out the window at my Oldsmobile. 'I'm afraid this means we may be bending the law a little.'

'Laws were made to be broken,' I tell him. 'It's the American way.'

23

Before going to my well-earned beauty sleep tonight I do a little straightening up in the living room where I discover the following letter buried underneath the usual stacks of junk-mail and psychic propaganda from Colonel Robert Roberston and his nutty followers.

Herewith it goes as follows:

Dear Emma

Thanks for your letter.

Please don't worry too much, and believe me when I say that Teddy can take care of himself. If he still hasn't shown up in a month, however, contact me c/o the Rama Life-Force Workshop in Taos, where I will be conducting a positive reinforcement seminar a few weeks from now. But please don't call. Either write or fax.

Obviously you have been dredging up the past a lot lately because you find the present state of existence too onerous and burdensome to live in. Has Dad changed at all? Probably not.

Please try to remind yourself that I am not a force in your past life. Only *you* are a force in your past life. Whatever traumas, tragedies or conflicts you attribute to our relationship are really just indications of the deep dissatisfaction you feel with your present state of being. This is perfectly normal, by the way.

The trickiest part about life is that we spend too much time living it to have any time left over for thinking about it. Working hard all day, fixing meals, bathing, watching really bad journalism on TV, and being regularly assaulted by carcinogens in our environment and so on. Partly this is the fault of the capitalist hegemony. But partly this is just the way cosmic existence operates all the time.

I guess I'm trying to tell you what you kept telling me so often when I was little (though I was too unenlightened to recognize your eternal wisdom at the time). 'Cassie,' you used to say. 'There's no use crying over spilt milk.'

I'm sorry for whatever memories you have of me that make you unhappy. I wish you long-life and well-being, but that doesn't mean I feel responsible for your spiritual inner conflicts, your loneliness, your sadness, or your really awful marriage.

Tell Dad I said hi.

Devotion, Obligation, Surrender,
Cassie

P.S.   Your letter made me cry. Please don't do it again.

That night I don't go to sleep for ages. Though I'm tired as a mule I can't seem to lie still for one minute, turning over and back and forth and readjusting my pillows and so on. It's as if Cassie's letter has stirred up something inside me, all whirling and itchy, memories that aren't just mental but physcial too, hiding down there in my body like termites or worms. Now they're all shook up and agitated. Now they'll never leave me alone.

Finally I fall asleep and suffer the strangest dreams. They are especially strange dreams because your horrible grandpa isn't in them, but only my big empty house, doors and windows staring at me, and me lost in the familiar corridors. Even though I'm not a trained psychotherapist, and I only read one book in my entire lifetime about interpreting dreams (it was written by the famous Sigmund Freud but I couldn't get through more than a couple boring chapters), I think this dream is pretty easy to interpret anyway.

In it (my dream, of course), I am roaming around inside my house and finding all sorts of strange rooms. This symbolizes how I've been opening all sorts of strange rooms and memories in my own body lately.

(This is just a basic dream-interpretation, by the way, so don't take it too seriously or anything.)

Then, when I start to get frustrated in these dark corridors I hear noises downstairs. I hear the picture window hissing open and shut. I hear the shovel scraping in the back yard, and someone breathing heavily.

So then I think: At last this dream's beginning to make sense.

Horrible old Marvin, I think. At it again.

A wonderful surprise awaits me, however. When I go downstairs to investigate, I find all the living-room lights on but no Marvin anywhere! Instead, who should I find sitting in the ugly old Barcalounger? Why, none other than my grandson Teddy, of course.

'Yo, Nana,' Teddy tells me. He is sitting way back in the Barcalounger, wiping his muddy hands on the legs of his blue jeans. The cuffs of his blue jeans are muddy, too, and rolled up a few notches. The mud on Teddy's clothing signifies all the dirty memories I have – not only about my crimes buried in the back garden, but about all the strange sexual thoughts that have been stirred up ever since I started 'dating' Mr Sullivan (to put it mildly).

'Can't sleep?' Teddy continues wiping his hands against his blue jeans, or wiping his sweaty forehead against the backs of his arms. He's rocking back and forth nervously, just like his mother used to whenever she ate too many candy bars. 'I can't sleep either. I'm like totally wired.'

I decide to confront my vision of Teddy and not run away. Maybe he's trying to tell me something important. Maybe he's even a representative of the spirit world, bringing me a message from my dead parents, or my dead sister Sophie.

133

'It took me ages to fall asleep,' I tell him. 'But finally I managed.'

Teddy is smiling at a far away point in space. The curtains are open on the picture window and all the porch lights are blazing. White light everywhere. So bright you can't see the moon or the stars.

(The back garden filled with light obviously symbolizes my fear of exposure for my vicious deeds. Though I guess this is a subconscious fear, since consciously the idea of being exposed for murdering Marvin doesn't bother me a whole lot. I killed the miserable bastard – so what?)

Teddy turns and looks at me. His muddy hands are tumbling over one another like playful little hamsters.

Teddy tells me, 'You're not going to believe what I just dug up in the back garden, Nana.'

And I tell him right back, 'You can never be too sure, Teddy. Maybe I *would* believe you, after all.'

24

Obviously things are moving rapidly onward towards their inevitable conclusion, so I better hurry up with my life story while I've still got one left to write about.

Here goes.

HOW I WOULD LIVE MY LIFE
ALL OVER AGAIN IF I COULD

(Including the last few weeks or so)
A personal Essay

by Emma O'Hallahan

Part I

The way I would live my life all over again if I had the chance would be to choose an entirely different set of parents. I know it's fashionable to blame all life's problems on your father and mother, but I'm not trying to be fashionable. I'm just trying to be honest.

I guess my father never meant to be the causer of pain and insecurities, and now that I think about it from my maturer (practically senile, in fact) perspective, I realize that most of the pain he caused was because he didn't have a very strong self-image rating – not in my book anyway. Well, if nothing else, he sure has passed his weak self-image rating onto this particular example of his progeny. Thanks, Pop.

From as far back as I can remember my sister and I competed for our father's attention and we both came up big losers, boy, did we ever. Our father had very few interesting things on his mind, and whenever he did have something interesting on his mind, it was usually something that made him angry at one of us.

'You know who you're both like? You're both like your goddamn mother, that's who you're both like,' our father could be heard frequently exclaiming in the Moriarty household, at least on those rare occasions when he said anything at all. 'All you ever think about is yourselves. You're not capable of love or affection, and if you weren't so selfish and irresponsible then maybe your mother wouldn't be such a terrible alcoholic and she'd spend more time taking care of us and less time sleeping around with every jerk in town. And you know what your *biggest* problem is? You have no sense of loyalty. Loyalty and devotion to myself, for example, who works his ass off all day bringing home the bacon, and taking care of both you and your mother. But do I receive one word of thanks or consideration? No, of course not. It's always your *mother* you go running to. It's always your *mother* who gets all the gratitude and love, while I'm slaving my life away at a lousy job, and getting screwed over by my local just because I missed a few days' work last month on account of my back.'

These were our father's comments, with which he tried to explain to my sister and I all our terrible shortcomings as human beings. These terrible shortcomings were made evident by the following examples:

1. We didn't clean our room properly.
2. We forgot to fix his dinner on time.
3. Whenever our mother found her way home we would take turns getting her undressed and putting her to sleep on the living-room sofa, and maybe we'd fix her breakfast in the morning, which our father took as a sure sign we loved her more than we loved him.
4. We interrupted him in the living room while he was watching TV.
5. We had terrible skin blemishes on our faces at dinner while

he was trying to digest his food. Our blemishes, he often told us, were the result of our 'bad attitudes' and 'selfish eating disorders'. In other words, if we weren't such rotten human beings on the *inside* we wouldn't look so ugly on the *outside*. (As I said before: Thanks again, Pop.)

6. We were often sad and depressed, or what our father used to call 'no fun to be around', usually because we were feeling guilty about our mother, or horrible about ourselves because neither of us was what you could call beautiful or especially intelligent.

Now, personally, I think maybe it was 'jumping the gun' a bit for our father to keep telling my sister and I how terribly selfish and thoughtless we were for forgetting to clean our room, or having the misfortune of feeling sad on a regular basis, or trying to keep our mother from falling asleep in the front yard so we wouldn't be embarrassed in front of our neighbors and school friends, but that was our father's opinion. Whenever he happened to be speaking to us, that is.

So getting back to my first point: I guess if I had it to do over again I would pick a different mother and father entirely. Mainly I would look for a reasonably happy couple, neither of whom would be committed to alcoholism. If I had to live with my real father all over again, though, I would probably try to give him 'a piece of my mind' every once in a while, and not skulk around the house constantly being afraid of him. Instead I would give him a little of his own medicine right back.

For example, I might say something to our father like the following:

'First off, Father, I'm sorry you're such a sad man. I wish you had a higher opinion of yourself so you could be successful with your life and not just mope around the house resenting yourself for your crummy job and horrible family. But I also think we should come to an understanding and we should come to this understanding pretty damn quick. Especially if you know what's good for you.

'For instance: If you want us to pick up our room, then tell us. If you want us to cook your dinner, we'll do the best we can to finish it in time for His Royal Highness when he gets off work. But if you don't like the way we look or feel or you don't like us trying to keep Mom off the front lawn then that's *your* problem. We know you work hard all day but we both work hard in school all day too, and then we have part-time jobs at the canning factory, so if you don't get dinner in time for your delicate digestive system – tough tamale.'

Like me, my sister married young to the first awful man who would take her away from San Pedro, and from the days of our respective marriages we hardly ever saw our father again. In fact, unless we called our father or came by his house we never heard a single word out of him. Not a postcard, not a phone call, not a shout out the window, nada. And whenever we visited he just sat in front of the TV pulling his lower lip and scratching himself. Even on the day of our mother's funeral, which was occasioned one night when our mother passed out, fell off the pier, and drowned. He didn't even bother to attend the funeral.

My older sister died in childbirth when her second son Ricky was born, mainly because I don't think she had proper eating habits or medical attention throughout her pregnancy, and her husband was a bully who pushed her around a lot, and of course our father never paid a single iota of attention to her after she left home, and so on and so forth. I guess I feel sorriest about my sister because there was something about our terribly unhappy parents which got in the way of our sisterly relationship, likewise.

Does that make sense?

Well, it sure as hell makes sense to me.

Part II

Good old Maudlin Self-Pitying Emma! Get me a big scratchy dish-towel before I spill tears all over the place.

Sometimes when I write about the past I get so deeply shaken I lose my breath, like there's been an earth tremor under my feet. Enormous forces rolling through the planet, lifting people up and putting them down again for no particular reason. I just sit here taking these big deep breaths and letting the air out in a rush. I feel I might even start hyperventilating while strange emotions expand in my face and chest.

But back to the subject of my 'personal essay'. When it comes to living my life all over again, I guess most of the things I'd change would be my upbringing and early environmental conditioning and so on. In more recent weeks, however, I have less things about my life I regret, which is not the same thing as saying I haven't made my fair share of mistakes.

On the mistakes front, I would probably correct the following which I've committed in the last few weeks or so:

1. I wouldn't have shot your grandpa in the back of the head, and if I had shot him in the back of the head I sure wouldn't have used a shotgun. Boy, you should have seen that mess.

What I might do next time (not that there'll *be* a next time) is either use a much smaller gun, or garrote him with piano wire. Or if I did use a shotgun I would first put him to sleep with sleeping pills. Then I would tie a big hefty trash bag over his head, so that when I shot him in the back of the head there wouldn't be so much bloody brain matter flying around. Then, after he was good and dead, I would just tie up the trash bag around his head with one of those handy little wire tie-strips that come with the trash bags. Then I would drag him out to the yard where his grave would be waiting for him very conveniently (since I would have hired a gardener to dig it many days in advance).

This, though, is all water under the bridge. Especially since if I had possessed the foresight to use sleeping pills and trash bags I could have just poisoned Marvin to death and avoided all sorts of unfortunate hassles. In fact, if I'd poisoned him, I might even have coaxed him out to the back yard during his fatal delirium, thus avoiding having to drag him out there myself. (I'm almost certain that's what happened to my back, come to think of it.)

But in the heat of the moment I did what was necessary, I guess, so now I have to live with it.

(I sure do remember spending all that morning cleaning the disgusting kitchen, however. In fact, there are still some places – like between the dishwasher and the refrigerator – I never did get to with either the mop or the sponge. And now, frankly, I'd just as soon not think about it.)

2. I wouldn't have killed Mrs Stansfield whatsoever, no matter how paranoid or delusory I got. Instead, I would have been as rude to her as she always was to me. I would have simply told her not to come around anymore and left it at that.

For example: 'Why don't you stop lurking around my back yard and go socialize with your real friends in the neighborhood, Mrs Stansfield? You know who I mean – all those lovely people with proper intelligence quotients and social backgrounds and so forth. Men and women who believe in feminist politics, and Neighborhood Watch programs, and the free-market economy and so on. But don't hang around my house anymore, Mrs Stansfield. Because if you don't like me, I probably don't like you *twice* as much.'

3. I wouldn't drink so much and I'd join a gym. Then maybe I wouldn't have gone completely around the twist and gotten myself in this big mess I can't seem to get out of.
4. I wouldn't have let Mr Sullivan get so heavily involved with me so quickly. (Poor Mr Sullivan!)
5. I would have 'opened up' more to Teddy since he came to visit, and told him all about our family history, especially about his mother, Cassie. Just yesterday at breakfast, for example, Teddy looked up from his Cheerios and asked me point blank:

'Nana, is it true that when Mom was only seventeen you and Grandpa paid a fifty-seven-year-old con-man named Raoul Stevenson five thousand dollars to take her away from home?'
And, of course, what could I tell him?
'Well,' I said. 'Not exactly.'
Then I took out the Oldsmobile and went to collect my packages from the Home Gardening Center.

25

Tonight after finishing my essay I come outside in the hallway and find all the lights are out. I can hear Teddy's little Walkman buzzing away behind his door. Mr Sullivan is snoring busily in the master bedroom, where I guess he sort of invited himself to stay the evening.

I go back to my office and unlock the gun cabinet. Down in the bottom drawers is what Marvin used to refer to as his 'heavy metal', which was never to be touched except in the event of a serious civil emergency, such as the one Marvin has been expecting ever since blacks and women got the vote.

I empty out one of Marvin's old banker's boxes. The banker's box contains lots of manuscripts with titles like 'The Death of Liberty', 'Tooth and Claw', and 'Savage Sunrise for Mankind'.

I toss Marvin's manuscripts onto the floor and stomp all over them.

'Happy Literary Immortality, Marvin!' I tell him as loudly as I can without waking Teddy or Mr Sullivan. 'Happy Literary Immortality to You!'

By the time I have hauled the banker's box full of 'heavy metal' out to the back garden Marvin is already waiting for me. I am finally beginning to get a sense of how Marvin's mind operates. Basically he just loves being wherever he's

141

not wanted. Which, so far as I'm concerned, is practically anywhere, anytime.

'Whatever happened to us, Emma?' Marvin asks me philosophically. He is standing with his hands on his hips, leaning back a little and gazing up at the stars. 'What happened to the sharing? The nurturing? The sense of two lonely human beings making their way together across this vast, blazing universe of loneliness and pain? Sure, we were never what you could call "in love" or anything. But we had something a lot better than love. We had mutual respect, Emma. We had a little something I like to call "a dialectic of trust".'

'I'd rather not talk about mutual respect and dialectics of trust right now,' I tell him. Then I overturn the banker's box and the large metal pipes and canisters tumble out with hard solid thuds.

Very solid, I think. Very dependable.

'But that's always been our problem, hasn't it?' Marvin turns to look abstractly at me over his shoulder. 'We always found ways *not* to talk about it. We learned a whole lot of complicated ways *not* to express how we felt. You see, Emma, I'm starting to understand things a lot better now that I'm dead. Maybe because understanding things is just about all I've got left to do anymore.'

Marvin gestures vacantly at the wide, messy yard, the bright stars and gleaming crescent moon. Suddenly Marvin doesn't look so old and decrepit anymore. In fact, he looks a whole lot younger and, well, I wouldn't exactly call it 'handsome' or anything, but a lot more *presentable* than he's *been* looking. His hair has gone back to the normal greasy color it was before we were married. His clothes are no longer rotting off him. And the loose parts of his face that were falling off just a few days ago are now back in their proper positions, with hardly any wrinkles or liver spots on them whatsoever.

While Marvin babbles on with all his stupid insincere apologies I am carefully dividing Marvin's armaments into three different categories on the dry lawn at my feet.

1. Hand grenades.
2. Cigar-box-sized demolition devices from many different countries (Chile, Germany, Russia and Belgium).
3. Unidentifiable pipes and canisters, all of which are filled with God only knows what sorts of explosive substances.

Marvin is staring at the stars again. The more solid and real things feel to me, the more abstract and dreamy Marvin starts to act. (This also strikes me as perfectly normal Marvin-like behavior, by the way.)

'We've put men on the moon,' Marvin says. 'We've explored the deepest depths of oceans. We've used microscopes and telescopes to penetrate atoms, stars, bodies and minds. It's not too much to ask, is it? For two caring adult individuals to sit down and just *talk* to each other for a few hours or so? To try straightening out all the hate and rage they feel inside? All the hurt. All the uncompromise. All the sad brutal regrets. I want you to know I'm willing to accept responsibility for my bad behavior over the years, Emma. I realize I may not have been the best husband in the world and I could be, you know, pretty stubborn sometimes. But if I do that, Emma, if I'm willing to admit some of *my* faults, then you've got to be willing to admit some of *your* faults as well. Maybe, Emma, just *maybe*, well, maybe you made *your* share of mistakes, too. Maybe *you* haven't been exactly the perfect *wife* or anything, either.'

This is so 'marvinish' I can't stand it. I am trying to locate the safety-switch on a Soviet TM-38 anti-tank mine but I'm not having much luck.

'Marvin,' I tell him, 'if you want to start admitting your failures as a human being, that's *your* business. But leave me out of it, will you?'

Marvin takes a long deep breath. After a moment, he shrugs a little.

'I was just trying—'

'I mean it, Marvin. I really do.'

I show him a pretty good-sized hand-grenade, which is slightly rusty around the casing, with white flaky bits of mineral deposits on the handle.

Marvin looks at me for a moment, then at the hand grenade. Then he looks admiringly at the various other armaments on the lawn at my feet.

'Jesus,' he says, 'I forgot about that stuff.' He hitches up his belt and pats his firm, youthful belly, which was a vain habit of his before he got tubby and old.

He seems very happy for a moment, like a child who's rediscovered forgotten toys in the basement.

'Maybe *you* forgot about this stuff, Marvin,' I tell him. 'But *I* sure as hell didn't.'

26

By the time I make my way back to bed it's almost four a.m. and I'm feeling very clear about things in my heart of hearts. Mr Sullivan is asleep in my bed, snoring loud enough to beat the band, and I take off my nightgown and try to slip between the sheets as quietly as possible.

But it's like setting off a kind of amorous land-mine. Mr Sullivan's body starts moving the moment my body hits the sheets.

'Hello, sweetheart,' Mr Sullivan says.

I push his hands away as politely as I can.

'Please, Mr Sullivan,' I tell him. 'I have a lot on my mind right now.'

Mr Sullivan just breathes real quietly for a few minutes. I can't help thinking back to the big empty hole Marvin dug for me in the back garden, which I have just finished loading up with the explosive supplies I purchased from Mr Rutherford's Home Gardening Center. I gathered the sticks of TNT into clumps and tied them together with lengths of Clover Brand Black Finish Safety Fuse. Then I crimped one end of fuse into one end of the central stick of each clump. (The official chemical name of these 'high explosives', by the way, is trinitrotoluene, or TNT. Try saying 'trinitrotoluene' six times fast without making a mistake!) Then I strung all the various armaments and TNT sticks around the yard, as if I was stringing up Christmas lights, along with various blasting caps looped together on lengths of black grainy detonating cord.

Mr Sullivan's hands come back to me again. A *bit* more respectfully, but not much.

'How about a little glass of brandy,' Mr Sullivan says, and of course I know exactly what *he's* got on his filthy mind. 'It might help you relax.'

I'm about as unrelaxed as an old girl gets. I remove Mr Sullivan's hands from my person for the second time.

'Brandy confuses me, Mr Sullivan, and I think you know that. I need to keep my mind straight for the next twenty-four hours or so. At least until I get some important writing finished in my journal.'

Mr Sullivan rolls onto his back and clasps his hands behind his head. He lets out a long 'hmmmmmm' sound, kind of like a closed-mouth yawn. I feel him drifting away already, forgetting I even exist. He is going away to some dream-world filled with exotic young girls who drink brandy whenever men ask them to, and none of them ever send 'mixed signals'.

Isn't that just like a man? Dream on, Mr Sullivan.

I feel terribly angry all of sudden, and I don't know whether I'm angry at Mr Sullivan for turning away from me the exact moment he realizes he's not getting all the 'mattress action' he requires, or if I'm just angry at Marvin (as per usual) for the same old boring reasons.

But whoever I'm angry at, one thing is certain. The only available object for me to train my anger on is, of course, the unfortunate Mr Sullivan.

'And another thing, Mr Sullivan. Maybe this isn't the right time to bring it up or anything, but I should tell you now while I've got the chance.'

I feel Mr Sullivan's eyes spring open. A sudden alertness activates in my dark bedroom which I can feel in my bones. It's like the way you can feel a pilot light ignite the burners in the water heater, even when the water heater is way downstairs in the basement.

'I don't mean to hurt you, Mr Sullivan.'

'Yes?'

146

'I don't mean to lead you on.'

'Yes?'

'I don't mean to send you a lot of mixed signals about our personal relationship, or where our relationship's going, or what sort of commitment I'm willing to make to you at this point in time.'

This time there's a much longer pause. Mr Sullivan is digesting. Mr Sullivan's mind is working really hard.

'So what are you trying to say, Emma?'

His body is stiff and heavy, pulling, pulling at me, at all the things I own, at everything I've ever known or been. Pulling me into it. Trying to make itself part of me.

'What I mean is I don't think we should be seeing each other anymore. I'm sorry, Mr Sullivan, but I'm afraid that's how I feel.'

Oh boy, did I make a *big* mistake.

Here I was trying to be kind and get Mr Sullivan out of my house as quickly as possible, and all I did was make a total mess of things.

Mr Sullivan didn't stop crying all night, which kept me up until dawn practically. I did manage to drift off for ten or fifteen minute intervals, during those periods when Mr Sullivan had decreased his emotional crisis to a mild sob. But then he would start crying and shaking and gasping for breath all over again, and I'd be awake again almost immediately.

'But I don't *want* to go!' Mr Sullivan would start crying again, completely out of nowhere. Then he'd pour more tears and snot into my clean towels and handkerchiefs, or tear through another box of my best Kleenex two-ply. 'I *love* you, Emma, and I don't *want* to go!'

So much for my good night's sleep, anyway.

'I know you love me, Mr Sullivan, and I love *you*. It's just I need a little more time to think things over, that's all. You don't have to go away forever. You can always come back, you know. Like maybe this weekend. Come over for the whole weekend and I'll fix us both a really nice steak.'

'But you said you wanted me to *leave*!' And Mr Sullivan

has rolled onto his side and started his monster crying-heaves again. Oh boy. All my life I kept saying I wanted a 'sensitive man', and now look at me.

By this time I don't *care* what I said. I just know I'm prepared to say *anything* if he'll stop yowling for two seconds.

But he doesn't stop yowling.

So I have to get out of there.

I go downstairs to fix breakfast and find Teddy eating a sweet roll and reading what looks like a comic book but which Teddy refers to as a 'graphic novel'.

'Yo, Nana,' he says. But he doesn't look up from his *Batman*.

'Yo, Teddy,' I tell him.

I check the curtain on the back window and see it's still closed all the way.

'Bit gloomy around here, isn't it?' Teddy says.

I pour Teddy some orange juice.

'I like a little gloom in the morning, dear. Now I'm about to fix Mr Sullivan eggs for breakfast. Would you like some?'

Teddy looks up. He is absently rubbing the corner of a book-page between his thumb and index finger.

'Did you lower the old boom on Mr Sullivan, Nana?'

'Whatever do you mean, Teddy?'

'I mean, did you hand him his walking papers? Did you disengage his leash? His yowling kept me up all night.'

I slice a chunk of butter into the saucepan. I take some eggs from the refrigerator and a Pyrex bowl from the shelf.

I try to be as forthright as possible. This is me: The New Emma. Full speed ahead and damn the consequences.

'I *am* married to your grandfather, Teddy. Mr Sullivan knew that when we started seeing each other. If he expects anything more from me than just casual friendship, he's simply not being realistic.'

Teddy considers this for a moment. Then he replaces his attention between the pages of his comic book.

Gently I crack the first egg and empty it into the thick Pyrex bowl.

'Yeah,' he says, 'I guess you're right, Nana. Depending, of course, on whether Grandpa and our former neighbor, Mrs Stansfield, are ever heard from again in the history of our planet.'

27

Dear Kids, Grandkids, etcetera, etcetera (see page 1).

Well, so much for the summing up of the deeds and thoughts of a lifetime. I did my best.

I never really did get around to straightening out things with our lawyer, Mr Spengler (at least not that I can remember) which makes this diary of major importance in a court of law. I, of course, want all our property divided equally between all surviving kids and grandkids. Please don't squabble over the nickels and dimes and try to enjoy yourselves with whatever money you end up with. This would mean a lot to me.

I guess the part about writing one's personal auto-biography which is most difficult for me is the 'form' part. Here I have told you my various crazy experiences over the last few weeks and decades, which is easy, but now comes the hard part. This means bringing all the random events of my life together into a stirring, meaningful conclusion (or what the French call a denouement), and what have I got to offer? I'll tell you what I've got to offer:

High explosives in the garden. Mr Sullivan crying his eyes out in the living room. My favorite daughter, Cassie, estranged from me for ever, probably even after I'm dead. Teddy so jaded by sex at the tender age of seventeen that all he does is masturbate, read comic books, and try to get me to 'open up', even though I'm afraid 'opening up' in a verbal sense belongs more to Teddy's generation than to mine. And as if that's not all, ten gallons of Unleaded gasoline in the garage (not to mention another five gallons or so under the back porch) which I still haven't figured out what to do with yet.

So I guess this is the time to thank all my guests, starting with some of the minor players first. For example, I'd very much like to thank Officer Rodrigues and his brief law-enforcement partner, Officer Lathrop, for helping me so much when I was attacked one night by a black burglar.

OFFICER LATHROP
(reading from his report)

Six feet or six three. Negro, gray slacks, white tennis shoes and wearing a ski mask.

ME

And of course, a special thanks to my always-hungry police-friend, Officer Rodrigues. Where would I have been without your frequent visits to my crazy household, Officer Rodrigues? You made me feel normal at a time when I needed that feeling very bad – boy, did I ever. Thanks for being there for me. Along with our mutual friends, the Stansfields. Mr and Mrs Stansfield, that is.

OFFICER RODRIGUES

Be careful with those detonators, Emma. You could lose fingers playing around with toys like that.

We are all sitting in a row of plastic, scoop-shaped chairs on the platform while the audience takes turns applauding each of my terrific guests. Mrs Stansfield gives the audience a little wave.

MRS STANSFIELD

No hard feelings, Emma. Have a great trip and I'll see you again real soon.

I turn to the happily applauding audience as the stage-lights start to dim.

ME

And of course where would we be without my extra-special guest-host all this week? You all know who I'm talking about – my best friend in the whole world, *Mr Mike Douglas*!

The audience goes wild.

MIKE DOUGLAS
(wearing his sincerest, most
basset-hound-like expression)

Why, thank you for having me, Emma.

Now I turn my chair to my main camera, and the lights go down on everybody but me.

EMMA

Now if you don't mind, I'd like to get serious for a moment and talk about a problem of concern to all Americans, young and old alike.

Marvin, sitting slumped in the front row with his usual bad attitude, turns rudely to the old woman sitting next to him (not that she's interested in his opinions even one iota) and says to her:

MARVIN

I really *hate* this part of the show.

But of course I'm too professional to let this one heckler ruin my final thought-provoking words for everybody, so I bravely continue.

EMMA

I'm talking, of course, about the problem of interpersonal family relationships.

I give Marvin a good hard look, just so he knows *I* know he's out there.

EMMA

As we all realize, interpersonal family relationships have long been a problem for all mankind. And why shouldn't they be? Just consider the possibilities. A group of men and women living together in the closest physical proximities. Sometimes sleeping in the same beds, sharing the same toilets and bathtubs. Eating together at the same table night after night, sometimes getting food on their faces, or making impolite, disgusting noises while they digest or masticate (i.e. chew). And this is just the basic *animal* problems of people living together! We haven't even *touched* upon the more serious psychological aspects, which can often be far more complicated altogether.

In the audience, Marvin is displaying his usual smirk and showing it around to all the other audience members (not that they're paying him any attention, of course.)

EMMA

People who get angry and hurt and emotionally unstable at the drop of a hat. People who are filled with their own selfish concerns all the time. People with nutty uncontrollable sexual desires, or chemical imbalances, or neuroses and bad behavior syndromes, or even what the younger generation simply like to call 'bad vibes'. Maybe hormonal maladjustments, or pimples and bad breath. Put all these people of various ages in a house together, and mix in all these various psychological infirmities and ailments, and you've got a pretty combustible combination. It's like, well, I guess it's a lot like pouring ridiculous amounts of TNT, dynamite, unleaded gasoline and other high explosives into a big hole in the garden and lighting a match. Imagine what would happen if somebody did a crazy thing like that!

In the audience, Marvin isn't used to being paid so little attention. He turns to the old lady next to him and says:

MARVIN

You know what I'd like to do to my own *personal* interpersonal family member, Emma O'Hallahan? I'd like to take a big fat piranha and shove it straight up her hairy backside!

Well, I don't have to tell you. After Marvin's crude words have finished echoing throughout our studio you can hear a pin drop. All the nice old ladies are looking at me with terribly shocked expressions on their features. Marvin is smirking and having a gay old time of it, and I know it would be a terrible mistake for me to ignore him any longer. I am captain of this particular ship, and its crewmembers depend for their safety and well-being on my quick wits and decision-making capacities.

Okay, Marvin, I think. Here goes.

EMMA
(turning to smug Marvin in the audience)

Well, Marvin, I guess you must be feeling pretty darned pleased with yourself about now. You've managed to interrupt me in the most important segment of my show, and you've even started upsetting the nice ladies of my audience with your vulgar speech patterns.

Marvin folds his arms across his chest, as if this will make him bigger and more solid-looking.

MARVIN

Well, I guess so, Emma. I guess I *am* feeling pretty darned pleased with myself.

It's pretty obvious by this point that I don't have much choice in the matter. I must face up to Marvin's cruel bullying on behalf of not only myself, but on behalf of my sorely tried audience members. What's more, the entire ugly incident is being captured on film for all posterity by our studio's various TV cameras. In other words, now you kids and grandkids can see for yourselves what it's been like living with your horrible grandpa: my sincerity and patience being constantly tested by Marvin's nastiness and evil-intentions.

I reach into my writing desk and remove the little 'last resort' I've been looking forward to all morning. It's not that little, actually, and takes both my hands to lift it. I show it to Marvin.

EMMA

What do you think *this* is, Marvin?

Marvin refuses to act concerned. He won't take his eyes off me.

MARVIN

What do *I* think it is, Emma? I think it's a Soviet TM-46 metal-cased anti-tank mine. I bought it three years ago through an ad I placed in *Soldier of Fortune Magazine*, which is, of course, my favorite over-the-counter magazine in the entire world.

Marvin thinks about this new information for a moment. Then he takes a quick glance at the round metal device which I have placed on my writing desk next to my loose-leaf diary. The round metal device looks like one of those camping cookery sets my son, Thomas, used to bring home whenever he and his friends were planning an overnight African safari in our back yard.

Marvin looks at me again.

MARVIN

You could blow quite a little tune on that sucker, Emma.

EMMA

And guess what sort of tune I'm intending to play, Marvin?

Marvin unfolds his arms and slowly shrugs his shoulders.

MARVIN

Would it have something to do with *me*?

EMMA

That's absolutely correct. I'm going to blow a little tune called 'What's left of Marvin?' Get the picture?

Marvin keeps shrugging and rolling his head around on his neck, like a sort of yoga relaxation exercise. Not that Marvin ever took Yoga, and certainly not that Marvin has ever known how to relax.

Suddenly I am distracted from Marvin's terrible rudeness

by noises outside in the hallway. I hear Teddy and Mr
Sullivan whispering out there and heading toward the
master bedroom.

MARVIN

So get on with your stupid speech, Emma. We haven't got
all eternity, you know. Don't you people ever break for a
commercial?

I get up from my chair and the studio cameras follow me
to my door. All the lights have been trained on the door,
so everybody in the audience, Marvin included, are now
cloaked in darkness.

Outside in the hallway, Teddy and Mr Sullivan are trying
not to make much noise, but I can still make out a few
words anyway.

TEDDY

Only for tonight. A little nap maybe. I'll take care of
everything.

MR SULLIVAN
(still snuffling away like a big baby)

I don't understand how. Maybe we shouldn't. How could
she ever. Why do I have to?

Once I'm certain all the lights have been turned off on the
audience behind me I open my office door.

Outside the hall is dingy and badly lit since I still haven't
replaced that fuse in the fuse-box. Out here dust motes are
swirling around and pale sunlight coming through the
bedroom windows. Teddy has one arm around the unfortunate Mr Sullivan and is showing him the guest room

157

where the single bed has been nicely made and the windows left open to catch a breeze.

                    EMMA

Teddy? What are you two doing out here?

                    TEDDY
              (slightly guilty-looking)

I'm putting Mr Sullivan down for a little nap, Nana.

                    EMMA

I thought I asked you to go for a walk in the park today?

                    TEDDY

Sorry, Nana. Mr Sullivan needs his beauty sleep. Then we'll both get out of your hair. I promise.

Oh boy. It's so hard to get angry at either of them.

                    EMMA

Okay, Teddy. But remember. I need the house completely to myself later this afternoon.

                    TEDDY

Cool, Nana.

The moment I close the door they start whispering again. Then I hear the door to Teddy's room open and close until I can't hear them whispering anymore.

MARVIN

We're waiting out here with bated breath, Donkey-Pustule.

All the lights have come back on, but wouldn't you just know it. Marvin has chased my entire audience away! In the big echoing TV studio there is nothing left but a few hundred empty metal folding chairs sitting with perfect posture like a chorus of glimmering, polite robots. Marvin is sitting alone in the empty front row with his arms folded. His smirk lights up like a big neon sign.

MARVIN'S SMIRK

You're a waste of attention, Emma. A waste. A big waste of attention.

EMMA

Nobody asked you, Marvin!

Marvin interrupts his smirk to say:

MARVIN

Here we go again. Major psychotic episode, take two.

EMMA
(refusing to let him get her goat)

It's not a psychotic episode, Marvin.

Marvin turns and points to my brandy bottle on the bookshelf.

MARVIN

There it is, Emma. Just one little drinky-poo? Come on, re*lax*.
It's probably the last drink of brandy-poo you'll ever have.

THE BRANDY BOTTLE

Drink me, Emma. Drink me, drink me, drink me, drink me,
drink me.

EMMA
(as solid as an oak)

Forget it, Marvin. I see what you're trying to do and I can
promise you one thing. It's *not going to work.*

I stand up from my desk and pick up the TM-46 anti-tank
mine, from which the grayish paint is flaking in places.
A hush falls over the crowd (even though I can't see
them).

EMMA

One more word out of either of you, Marvin, and I'm
blowing us *all* to kingdom come!

The brandy bottle shuts up immediately. Marvin, of course,
takes a little longer to get the picture.

MARVIN

Well, well, well. So you're going to blow us all to smither-
eens, are you?

EMMA

You can bet your bottom dollar, Marvin.

MARVIN

Does that mean you're going to *follow through*, Emma? Does that mean you're finally going to finish something you've *started*? *You*, Emma O'Hallahan, *finishing* something you've *started*?

Suddenly I get a terribly queasy sensation in my stomach.

EMMA
(hesitantly)

I finish a lot of things I start, Marvin. You don't have any right to say that.

Marvin has that look in his eyes again. Even when I know I'm right I can't keep being right so long as Marvin's got that look in his eyes.
If I'm going to continue being who I am then I have to keep talking. To remind myself what I sound like. To remind myself who I am.

EMMA

I've given birth to two children, Marvin. I've raised them into adults with families of their own, however dysfunctional. I've kept this house in order, and managed to be civil to my neighbors (most of them, anyway), and done all the shopping and gardening. In recent days I've even kept a diary of my thoughts and activities, and I'm doing the best I can to arrange my financial affairs so our descendants won't have to fight over their inheritance for eons. You have no right to say I've never finished anything, Marvin. I'm about to finish a *lot* of things. In fact, I'm about to finish everything so totally and completely that I'll never have to finish anything else ever again!

Everything goes suddenly quiet in the room.
Outside in the hall, I hear somebody breathing.

MARVIN

It's the coppers, old girl. And you know what they're saying to themselves? They're saying, 'I think it's time for this lady's medication.'

The door opens and I turn.

Teddy is wearing his cuffed baggy corduroy short pants and his *other* lime green T-shirt. This lime-green T-shirt has a faded decal of a psychedelic surfboard over the top pocket, and under the surfboard it says:

AVILA BEACH, CALIFORNIA

Home of the Boogie Board

TEDDY

Nana, can we talk?

In the background, just to see if he can make me lose my temper in front of Teddy, your horrible grandpa continues spewing his nasty lies and distortions.

MARVIN

You keep talking about how much you've *finished*, Emma, when we both know for a fact that you've never finished *anything*. Your kids aren't talking to you. Your marriage ended in multiple-homicides. You have no idea *in the world* how to end your stupid diary. You don't even have the balls to end your affair honestly with your highly esteemed sex-slave, Mr Sullivan, who's presently crying his tiny little eyes out in *my* gun-room across the hall.

I take a long deep breath. I clear my mind of Marvin's horrible yelling. I look at my grandson.

EMMA

I thought we *agreed* you would leave me a little time to myself, Teddy. Not that I want to make you feel unwelcome or anything.

Teddy looks down at his wrinkled desert boots.

TEDDY

Nana, are you *sure* you don't need to talk? It's not good for your pores to keep everything bottled up inside. And if you don't sweat properly, you put extra pressure on your liver.

EMMA
(short but without being rude)

I'll take care of my own liver, Teddy. But thank you for being concerned.

Teddy shrugs, and starts to move back through the door. Then he thinks better of it.

TEDDY

Nana, can I just ask one little favor?

EMMA

What's that, Teddy?

Teddy cocks his head to one side and looks me in the eye.

TEDDY

Do you think you could stop scribbling in your diary for just two seconds when I'm trying to talk to you?

Suddenly I feel deeply ashamed. I put down my ball-point and place my hands on the table. I feel the words in my diary resonating against my fingertips. I feel very strange without my pen in my hand.

EMMA

You're absolutely right, Teddy. It's terribly rude of me and I'll stop. But can I ask you a favor in return? Can I *please* have a little more privacy this morning? Then I'll come down later and fix us both a nice hot lunch.

Teddy gives me a mock salute.

TEDDY

Cool, Nana.

When Teddy closes the door I'm just at the point of reminding him for the umpteenth time not to go out in the back yard, but by now I don't know why I should bother. I guess it's time to start trusting fate, especially since fate has been pretty good to me lately.

MARVIN

If weenies like your Mr Sullivan had anything to say about it, Emma, we'd all be living on collective farms, playing balalaikas and eating potato stew. You know what kind of world we'd have if your sex kitten was in charge of things, Emma? A world of *drones*! A world of bureaucratic bun-blisterers! A world populated by nothing but brain-starved, protein-deficient, gristle-chewing zombies – a world, in fact, much like the world we're living in *today*! Only you know what makes *our* world better than that, Emma? I'll tell you what makes it better. Individuality. That's right. The survival of the fittest through adaptation. Glorious mutation, Emma. Free enterprise and the right to bear firearms. And thank

God for the right to bear firearms, Emma. Because when your friend Mr Sullivan becomes World Leader of the Drone-Hordes, he and his kind will come marching straight over to my house to *try* and make me one of them. But I'm sure as hell not going along quietly – nosireebob. In fact, I'll be taking a few hundred of those drooling vegetable hordes with me – and *that's* a promise.

Oh boy oh boy oh boy oh boy. Listening to Marvin is like listening to a broken record. Only a broken record doesn't fill you with such an irresistible desire to blow its brains out with a shotgun and bury it forcibly in the garden.

I get up from my chair. My backside is sore, and my hand is sore as well from so much writing. I reach out for the Soviet TM-46 anti-tank mine. I don't feel in such a hurry anymore. I know by this point that fate will take care of everything.

EMMA

I wouldn't worry so much about the Brainless Hordes, Marvin. Because first you've got *me* to deal with.

Suddenly in the distance I hear my front doorbell starting to buzz.

MARVIN

If you could just finish *one* thing, Emma. If you could just finish *one* thing you've started.

The doorbell buzzes again and I put down my anti-tank mine. I ask myself: Isn't Teddy going to get it?

MARVIN

For example, Emma. In your diary you have repeatedly ridiculed my articles about improving the American Way of

165

Life. But whenever *you* try to write down a list of problems with our American Way of Life, you can't even finish it. What did you get, Emma? Nine out of ten? You couldn't even come up with one more *tiny* little suggestion for improving this great, crumbling nation of ours. If you're so smart, Emma, then why don't you come up with one more problem that needs to be corrected? One more problem which is causing our country to suffer total economic and moral collapse during our lifetimes.

The buzzer goes off again. And then again. Buzz buzz. Buzz buzz buzz buzz.

EMMA
(afraid to go too far towards the door)

Teddy?

MARVIN

Name *one* more little problem, Emma.

Marvin goes to the bulletin board and takes down my list. He puts it on the table in front of me and he's right. I've got nine problems listed, but ten numbers where problems should be put. I haven't finished it. I haven't even finished my list about What's Wrong with America.
Marvin hands me my ball-point.

MARVIN

Come on, old girl. Name *one* major problem with America, you old cud-chewer. Is it the rising national deficit? Eighty jillion trillion dollars or something – and still climbing? Is *that* what's wrong with our country, Emma? The rising national deficit?

I don't have to listen to this. Instead I listen to the front

doorbell ringing downstairs. Buzz buzz buh-buzz buzz.
Buzz buzz.

EMMA
(steadfastly)

No, Marvin. It's not the stupid deficit, whatever the hell
that is. It's not the eighty jillion trillion dollars.

Marvin leans into me, breathing mildew and fertilizer in my
face. His features are all corroded and distorted again. An
ear's falling off. A big worm's crawling out of his eyeball.

MARVIN

Maybe it's the federal justice system. Maybe it's all those
felons and murderers and sex offenders being put out on
parole. What about the federal justice system, Emma? Why
don't you write *that* down as number ten on your list? The
overly lenient federal justice system which lets murderers
and rapists out on parole so they can murder and rape
again. How does that sound, Emma? Does that sound like
what's wrong with America or what?

EMMA
(even more resolute)

No, Marvin. That's not it at all.

MARVIN

What about the tax laws, Emma? What about the crumbling
infrastructure? What about the inner cities, or the total
collapse of our American two-party political system?

EMMA

No, Marvin. No, no, no, no.

MARVIN

What about eastern Europe? The unravelling Soviet block. Jihads in the Mid-East. Iranians and the Hizbollah. What about South Africa, Emma? And while we're at it, what about the very strong possibility that someday, when we least expect it, we might even be invaded by aliens from outer space?

EMMA
(almost tired of saying it)

No, Marvin. You've got it all wrong. That's not what's wrong with America. That's not what's wrong with America at all.

Marvin stands up, clods of dirt and sluggish pale things falling across my desk and face. He looks all rotted and decomposed, just the way he's *supposed* to look, thank God. And no matter how awful he looks, he still looks exactly like who he's always been.

MARVIN

Why don't you tell me then, Emma? Why don't *you* tell *me* what's wrong with America? What's wrong with it, old girl? If you're so much smarter than me why don't you come up with just one more thing that's wrong with America? I *dare* you, Emma. I *dare* you to come up with just one more thing.

By now the buzzer downstairs is going, going, going and I know it will never stop, for ever and ever, like a fire alarm in hell. Somebody coming to visit but nobody in the entire house will ever let them in.

I'm not even angry. I don't even shout. I don't even tell Marvin with my lips – he wouldn't listen anyway. I just snatch my ball-point out of his hands and wipe off the fungus with a clean tissue. Then I pick up my list entitled

What's Wrong with America. Everything is perfectly simple. We're almost at the end of my story now.

EMMA

I'll tell you what's wrong with America, Marvin. I'll tell you what's wrong with America right this very minute.

Then, without further ado, I write down at the bottom of my list.

WHAT'S WRONG WITH AMERICA

10. Marvin's what's wrong with America! Marvin's what's wrong, Marvin, Marvin O'Hallahan is! It's *Marvin* that's wrong, it's *Marvin* that's wrong! It's you, it's you, *it's you*!

28

By the time I get downstairs the front doorbell has been ringing for ten or fifteen minutes without stop. Teddy is sitting in front of the TV watching *Wheel of Fortune*, where somebody is in the process of buying a vowel.

Teddy turns and looks up. He's twisting his right side-burn between his thumb and index finger. He doesn't look me in the eye, but he doesn't seem embarrassed or ashamed of me, either. He seems very far away, revisiting places in his mind that I've always wanted to visit just once.

'I think someone's at the door, Nana.'

At first I think I should probably get mad, but seeing Teddy so peacefully watching TV makes me feel kind of peaceful, too. In comparison to Teddy's happy space-stare, all I can remember is how Marvin used to act whenever the night-time version of *Wheel of Fortune* came on.

'Buy a vowel?' he'd start shouting at the drop of a hat, flinging his newspapers in the air or hurling his empty soda cans at the TV screen. 'You want to *buy* a vowel! How many goddamn vowels *are* there, for Christ's sakes! A, E, I, O, U! Here, *I'll* sell you a vowel! You give me three hundred bucks and *I'll* sell you a vowel, you stupid cow! Come right over here and sit on old Marvin's nether regions – that's right. And I'll give you an "Oh!" *That's* exactly the kind of vowel *I'm* going to give *you*.'

Buzz. Buzz buzz buzz buzz.

Whoever's visiting is definitely the most patient doorbell ringer I've ever encountered in my entire lifetime.

I go to the door, performing a few involuntary motions to make myself presentable. I pat my hair. I adjust my bra straps. I touch the corners of my mouth, scraping for food particles.

Not that there's very much you can do for your appearance at my age!

Oh, well.

I open the door and a big fat slab of sunlight falls across me. It lands on the hall carpet with a soft humming sound.

The stranger stands in the brilliant, foamy white light. His hands are yellowish and perfectly manicured. He's wearing a three-piece Brooks Brothers suit, a solid gold watch chain, flashing cufflinks and shiny patent leather shoes. His wiry gray hair is tied back in a thick pony-tail and he smells like daffodils. I can't see his face because of the sun, but I sure hear his voice clearly enough, round and stony and deep.

'Good morning, Emma. Do you recognize me? Do you know who I am?'

Of course I know. I can't even see him clearly and I know.

'Most people know me as Colonel Robert Robertson, sole-founder and proprietor of the Church of Immaculate Reason in Anaheim. But you may remember me as somebody else entirely. Do you, Emma? Do you remember?'

He comes through the doorway, eclipsing the bright sunlight. He's here. The last person I ever expected to see again and he's here. The same green eyes. The same placid, fair complexion. But more wrinkles, of course. More wrinkles for all of us.

It's me,' he says, reaching out his hands, as if he's about to take me waltzing off across the dance floor to the tune of twinkly harpsichords and sunny clarinets. 'Your daughter's old boyfriend, Emma. Your daughter's old boyfriend, Raoul.'

Cassie never told me, Teddy never told me, even your horrible, nasty, smelly old grandpa never told me. And now, just when nobody *needs* to tell me, somebody does. And just at the point when Teddy's about to tell me I'm wishing he wouldn't. I'm wishing *I* could tell *him*.

'Oh my God!' Teddy shouts from behind me. 'Look, Nana – it's *Dad*!'

29

'You know what money teaches you?' Raoul tells us later in the kitchen. 'That money doesn't matter. You know what living teaches you? That life's not the only experience you'll ever undergo. You know what you learn from your own two eyeballs and ears, your own private sensory assembly of tongue and nostrils and hands? That the world's filled with an infinity of things you'll *never* understand. I hate to get philosophical on you so early in the day, but think about it, the raw ornery contradictoriness of, well, *everything*. Light and darkness. Being and non-being. Yin and yang, mortgages and foreclosures, monuments and ants. Life is always in a process of negating itself, because that's what life *is*, see. A furious process of negating everything it isn't. Rude elemental matter. Physics bristling in the darkness. Other carnivores roaming in the night. I guess you could say I've learned a lot about myself over the years and sure, money was *part* of it. But it wasn't the *raison d'être* of old Raoul's existence, not by a long shot. Just because money's always taken care of me doesn't mean that I've ever cared for money.'

While I'm busy at the breadboard slicing assorted cheeses, processed meats and garnishes, Raoul is sitting at the table with Teddy, Mr Sullivan and Officer Rodrigues. All the windows are still curtained on the back yard, but I've uncurtained a few windows on the front. The house seems very shadowy and expectant, as if it's waiting for someone to arrive at any moment with a match.

Teddy finishes shuffling the cards and begins to deal.

'There's like only one game I know that you can play with four people,' Teddy says, with an unconvincing little shrug. 'And that's Go Fish.'

Office Rodrigues peers at Raoul as if he's sighting him through the lens of a rifle.

'That doesn't really answer my question, Raoul. I mean, you don't have to be specific or anything. Just last year, for instance. How much money did you pull in *last* year? Gross, not net.'

Raoul picks up his cards and begins sorting.

'You think it's money you want,' he says, 'but then as soon as you get it? Well, you immediately start trading it away for things. Food, clothes, holidays, retirement funds, houses, beach resorts, gambling casinos, you name it. And then there's the *family*. Six kids from four ex-wives, all boys.'

Raoul reaches out for Teddy's head but Teddy ducks and scowls.

'Of course, you always love the one who gives you the most trouble,' Raoul tells everybody. 'But that doesn't mean he doesn't still really piss you off.'

'First play goes to left of the dealer, Dad,' Teddy says. 'That means you.'

'Has . . .' Raoul glances around the table, click click click, like one of those video monitors in a bank. 'Mr Sullivan,' he decides. 'Has Mr Sullivan got a . . . *ten*?'

'Oh shit,' Mr Sullivan says. 'I've got three tens.'

Meanwhile, Officer Rodrigues hasn't even looked at his cards.

'Are you going to tell us how much you made last year or not?' He seems a little out of temper – which is, I guess, Officer Rodrigues's normal mode of being. Always just a little out of something. 'I figure it's billions. I figure it's like the gross national product of Costa Rica. I see your books in every supermarket and dime store in the county. I see your ads in every magazine, even *Playboy*.'

Teddy says, 'Nana, why don't you just nuke a few of our freeze-wrapped sandwiches in the microwave? There must be a whole drawer-full in there.'

'I need to keep busy,' I tell him. 'Nervous habit.'

Then I bring down the white ceramic plates and begin serving.

'Money's just something I call a "mediation metaphor",' Raoul tells them. 'In one of my recent books, *Pulling the Cosmic Trigger*, I described a "mediation metaphor" as, to put it in the simplest possible terms, the idea of something you don't have which you use to explain to yourself something that you'll never understand.'

'Those are the simplest possible terms, Raoul?' Officer Rodrigues is continually sorting his cards, as if he's trying every possible sequence in a mental combination lock.

'Let me put it *this* way,' Raoul says, pulling himself up to the table with a little swagger. 'How do we go about understanding the mysteries of our own bodies and hearts? Rage, love, laughter, oogenesis, indigestion, fatigue, body odor, regret, memory and desire? Why, we tell ourselves *stories*, stories about who we've never been and places we'll never go. The big bang, gangsters on Mars, nuclear fission, cowboy campfires, crimes in the streets, the sperm and the egg. We are story-making entities, ladies and gentlemen, because our minds are constantly translating our most intimate physical realities into poems, books, screen adaptations, letters to Mom. The commercials on TV – those are stories. The advancements of science – those are stories too. Going to the grocery store, eating a donut, picking your nose and tying your shoes – stories stories stories. So that's what I mean by a "mediation metaphor". Any piece of language we use to rationalize our world and make it make sense. Oh, and I'm sorry, Teddy. Did you say something?'

'Sixes, Dad. I asked you like three times already. I want all your sixes.'

'Hmmm.' Raoul plucks his walrus moustache and scans his fan of cards. He looks at Teddy a little bit the way I looked at Teddy the first day he got here.

'And if I perhaps actually *have* some of these hypothetical sixes you're looking for, son? Am I supposed to give them to you?'

'That's how the game works, Dad.'

Teddy uses the word 'Dad' with a little emphasis, like a particularly rude form of punctuation.

Officer Rodrigues, meanwhile, is still trying combinations on his secret interior lock.

'All well and good, Raoul,' he says. 'All well and good. So what I'm asking again is how *much*? How many mediation metaphors have you collected in your personal savings and checking accounts over the last year or so, or ever since the Church of Immaculate Reason went international? I hear you're cleaning up in Orlando. I hear you've opened Clarification Centers in Tokyo, Bhopal, and Washington DC.'

I bring them toasted sandwiches. I bring them sliced green apples and pears. I bring them milk for their coffee and ashtrays for their cigarettes. I feel like I'm filling up an enormous balloon with hot air. The balloon keeps getting bigger and warmer. It's lifting itself up off the ground. Eventually the balloon will go away and take care of itself.

And then, all of a sudden, my job here is done.

'I don't get it,' Teddy says. 'I've asked everybody for sixes and there's still one missing.'

As I take my bag from the counter, Teddy adds, '*Dad?*'

'Let me understand this. If I have more than one six, I have to give you *all* of them?'

Teddy turns to the other men at the table.

'I probably should have warned you right off the bat. Dad cheats at *everything*.'

I take my bag to the stairs. On the TV, Trish is saying to her long-time lover, Jack McIntosh, 'Sometimes I'm afraid people expect too much from each other. After all, we're just animals, aren't we? Just selfish animals worried about our own bellies and backs.'

I'm halfway up the stairs when I notice the silence in the kitchen. It emerges from the floors like a gigantic white iceberg.

I pause on the stairs. I wonder what time it is.

'Nana?' Teddy's voice initiates a brief flurry of whispers. I hear the coffee pot clatter on the stove. The gas jet ignites with a sudden muffled pop.

'Yes, Teddy?'

'Would you like to join us? I'm about to whip Dad's butt. And when I do we'll play another round.'

Do I want to join them? How strange.

'No, thank you, Teddy,' I tell him. 'I have a little cleaning to do in my office, and a little gardening left in the back yard.'

By the time I return downstairs they're at it again.

Officer Rodrigues: 'If *I* was making buckets of money, *I* wouldn't be ashamed to say how much I *made*.'

Mr Sullivan: 'What's it mean when you don't have any cards left?'

Raoul: 'Look, I got what I wanted. I went fishing and I got what I wanted.'

Teddy: '*Dad*. I asked if you'd talked to *Mom* lately. Jesus. Don't you ever listen to *anything* I say?'

Noise and confusion and anger, I think. And it seems to make them all so very happy together.

My TM-46 anti-tank mine feels as light and fluffy as a pillow. On my way through the living room I take my bottle of brandy from the mantelpiece.

One little sip certainly won't hurt me now.

'Nana?'

Teddy's voice has followed me out here into the living room.

'Yes, Teddy?'

'Are you *sure* you won't join us?'

The sunlight is everywhere.

'Maybe in a little while, dear.'

Then I step outside into the garden.

Raoul is saying: 'Well, I didn't actually *invent* "Divine Cybertronics". In fact, many ideas of the Church of Immaculate Reason were lifted freely from a science fiction paperback I discovered twenty years ago in a public laundromat. It was entitled *Journay Across the Black Atom*, and was written by a little-known hack writer named Stanley F. Templeton, a Polish-American in New Jersey who owned a dry-cleaning store and wrote galaxy-spanning science fiction in his spare time. Templeton originated the idea of the "foreign entity displacement effect". He originated the ideas of "interstellar resonance", "radical subjectivity" and "goal clarification". But while the totally forgotten Stanley F. Templeton may have originated many of the ideas of Divine Cybertronics, *I'm* the one who developed them into a workable *system*. And if you don't think that system works, why, just ask my accounts secretary how much we made last year. Sometimes I can't believe it myself.'

'I'm asking *you*,' Officer Rodrigues says. 'And I've *been* asking you for the past half-hour or so.'

Outside in the garden I am greeted by practically everybody. Marvin and Mrs Stansfield sunning themselves in green fiberglass lawn chairs. Mom and Pop, who are dressed much like they were in some long ago Thanksgiving dinner of my imagination, neither of them drunk for the first time in a million years probably. Even my budget assortment of kids and grandkids are there, sitting very politely on the edge of the patio with their hands in their laps and smiling.

'Let's just say *lots*,' Raoul says in the kitchen. 'Lots and lots and lots and lots.'

Marvin doesn't look so out of temper as usual. He visors his eyes with one hand and peers up at me, as if he's scouting for planes.

'I always did like that crazy Raoul,' Marvin says.

'Goodbye, Emma,' everybody says, my family and neighbors and local merchants, even a few old friends from high school. 'Take care. Don't forget to write.'

The sunlight is dazzling, like a sort of recognition. I walk up to the big hole Marvin has dug for me in the yard. The hole is very deep and black. Impossible to see into with so much sunlight everywhere.

In the kitchen Raoul continues to hold court. 'Just

imagine the miracle of your own body,' he is saying. 'It manufactures blood cells, for Christ's sake. It converts oxygen into life. It feeds an infinity of tiny micro-organisms, parasites, bacteria, enzymes. It's an entire world unto itself. It's scary, really. Life is everywhere.'

Well, kids, I guess this is the part where I'm supposed to sum things up and tell you my moral, but I'm afraid I'm not going to be able to do either. I'm standing on the rim of the hole Marvin dug for me in the ground. I'm holding the TM-46 anti-tank mine against my chest like a life-preserver. I am very, very tired of writing. This is the last diary I'm ever going to keep in the history of the entire Universal Consciousness.

Bye, bye, Universal Consciousness. Time for the Big Finale.

'No hard feelings, old girl.'

Your horrible grandpa has to get the last word in, of course. And by this point I don't even care anymore. Once you feel secure in your own individuality you don't care about silly things like who gets the last word in.

I am leaning forward. I close my eyes. I wonder if I'll hear anything? Probably not.

(I'd hit the deck, Teddy, if I were you.)

'I mean seriously, Emma. I certainly have no hard feelings. Do you have any hard feelings left against me?'

My feet are slipping against the edge of the hole. This is all much simpler than I ever dreamed possible.

'Screw you, Marvin,' I tell him.

Then I am flying through the air.

And finally I've figured out the perfect ending for my book.

December

19 December

Dear Mom

Teddy here, reporting in. Remember me? Your son.

I hope this comes through okay. Or are you so busy basking in cosmic emanations that you've neglected to check your office fax?

Wouldn't surprise me one bit.

Since we talked on the phone last night this place has been really hopping (in fact, Nana's house is a place which is pretty hopping generally – at least since I got here, anyway).

First off, Nana's feeling a lot better, even though she's still in traction at Orange County Hospital, and I doubt she'll ever do the bossa-nova again. They've got her doped up on some weird medication I wouldn't mind a little taste of myself. During visitors' hours today I sat in on a round-table discussion panel between Nana, Grandpa, you, Uncle Thomas, Jack the Insurance man, someone named Sophie, and someone else named Mike Douglas. Though of course Nana was moderator and the hospital room was totally empty except for her and me.

'That's very good medication,' the nurse said admiringly when she came in to check Nana's pulse.

'You're telling me,' I said.

While Nana's in the hospital I've been taking care of her house. I've paid her bills (many of which contained warnings from collection agencies or even pretty urgent-looking disconnection notices) and I've watered the lawns. Watering the lawns, however, doesn't really solve anything so far as the back yard's concerned, since the back yard has been one holy mess ever since I got here. What I've done so far is filled in the hole Nana dug, and taken all the rusty shovels and digging paraphernalia back into the garage. And of course I've hauled all of Grandpa's old army-surplus scrap metal out to the police weapons dump in Sepulveda (with the help of Nana's friend, Officer Rodrigues, of course).

'It seems your Nana has been a little confused lately,' Officer Rodrigues told me during our drive in Nana's Oldsmobile.

(By the way, I didn't tell Officer Rodrigues I don't have a license. Between you and me, okay?)

'Maybe not confused, exactly,' I told him. 'Maybe just a bit too overly industrious.'

I mean, if *I'm* not going to stick up for Nana, who will? I just hope that when I'm a senile old bat I'll have a similarly terrific grandson who takes wonderful care of me, likewise.

Actually I've grown pretty fond of Nana over the past week or so. She seems very weirdly unconcerned with material things like money, looks or appearances. And she's such a wonderful hostess that her place is constantly being visited by a whole variety of local freeloaders, such as myself, who appreciate her sandwiches.

Speaking of freeloaders, Dad arrived yesterday afternoon, just before Nana took a flying nose-dive into her budget abyss (clutching, by the way, her trusty loose-leaf notebook, in which she's been scribbling away to beat the band lately). It seems that Dad has become extremely concerned about Nana's and Grandpa's well-being, especially since he possesses a copy of Grandpa's Last Will and Testament which he's been waving around at everybody for the past two days. As I understand it, this Last Will and

Testament leaves all Grandpa's cash and liquefiable assets (with the exception of the house) to Dad's Church of Immaculate Reason in Anaheim.

When I arrived at Nana's hospital room this morning Dad was trying to get Nana to sign some legal papers attached to a wooden clipboard.

'Here you go, Emma,' Dad was saying. 'You sign this little paper for me and we'll ask our favorite nurse to come give you a little more of your fine medication.'

Nana was saying, 'Let me at that ball-point. I'll tell you what's wrong. I'll tell you what's wrong with America.'

When I came into the room Dad looked up at me very pleasantly. He seemed happy that we could share this delightful time together.

He nodded in Nana's general direction.

'She needs a lot of caring right now,' Dad said. 'She needs a lot of loving. She needs to feel part and parcel of a community to which she truly belongs.'

'She's already got a home, Dad,' I told him. 'A nice big ranch-style four-bedroom in Orange County.'

Dad turned and looked right through me at the blue sky in the window.

'Son,' he told me, 'some people need more than a big house to be happy. Some people need positive reinforcement stereotypes or high conceptual goal orientation procedures if they want to be *truly* happy.'

Dad blinked moistly. It was the first time I ever realized that not only can Dad still hurt me, but I can still hurt him, too.

So I told him. I told him point-blank.

'There's no money, Dad,' I said. 'And Grandpa's not dead, I don't care what Nana told you in her letter. And anyway, there isn't any money left, because Grandpa took it with him when he hit the road with his middle-aged sweetheart from next door. So you and the Church won't be receiving any inheritance, I don't care how many exorbitant lawyers you send over trying to get Nana to sign things. And as for your high-priced tort, Mr Spengler, well. I never saw him and Nana never saw him. Maybe you should check with your Accounts Department. My guess is that Mr Spengler's in Rio with *your* insurance premiums.'

Nana, meanwhile, was trying to snatch the ball-point pen out of Dad's hands. She was wearing one of those long pullover white cloth robes hospitals make you wear. She looked like a kitten slapping at flies.

'Marvin's what's wrong,' Nana said. 'Marvin's the *real* problem.'

'No money,' Dad said. He seemed to deflate with a long, subsiding hiss as if the air was being let out of all his tires simultaneously. 'No money, no inheritance, and no sign of Mr Spengler. Well, I'll be goddamned.'

Dad sat down in a red plastic chair. He was gazing off into space, as if anticipating the arrival of some tardy inspiration. I almost felt sorry for the guy.

So I gave Nana the ball-point and a few sheets of white foolscap attached to Dad's clipboard. Then I tore Dad's superannuated legal documents crosswise, and crosswise again.

Then I dropped them in the trash on my way down the hall for a sip of cold water.

(I didn't want to be there, you see? It's what Dad does that always hurts most and I'm terrified he'll recognize it someday. Because if Dad recognizes the hurt he makes me feel, then that will make the hurt more real. It won't be my secret anymore. It would be like giving Dad a gift of my pain – and frankly I don't think Dad deserves that much attention.)

So, while I was down the hall stealing a sip of water, Dad did what Dad has always done best.

He split.

When I got back to Nana's room she was asleep with the clipboard clutched to her chest in the exact same manner she was clutching the blue loose-leaf notebook yesterday morning when Mr Sullivan and I pulled her out of that big hole she dug in the yard. Gently I disengaged the clipboard from Nana's hands and placed the ball-point pen on the table beside her bed.

On the top sheet of white foolscap Nana had sketched the following diagram:

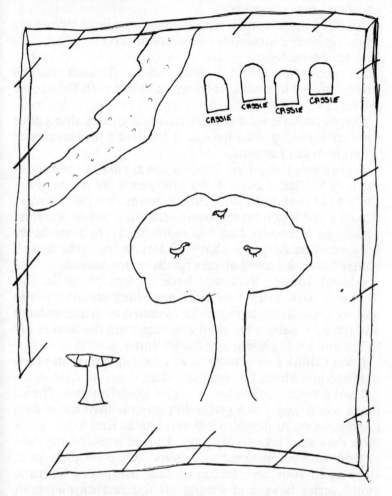

Well, Mom, what do you think? Are you flattered? I sure as hell would be.

I remember once when you were expounding pretty angrily about Grandma and Grandpa and 'What They'd Done To You' etc. that you told me: 'Regret doesn't matter.

I don't care how much my mother *regrets* what she did. Because regret isn't love. Regret doesn't make up for all the love I never received.'

All this from a woman who claims she's eliminated anger from her body's metabolic mood-enhancers!

Yeah, Mom. Sure.

Do you know what I think, Mom? I think anger's something we live with when we can't live with the people we love.

I loved Dad, remember? I loved him for years after I gave up ever knowing who he was. I felt Dad's presence even when he wasn't around.

I loved you too, Mom, but you always got in the way of my love for Dad. I guess it was pretty easy for you to get in the way of Dad, huh, since he was never around? I always thought that if you moved over just a *few inches* to one side, I might be able to see Dad a *bit* more clearly. I guess I never fully appreciated you – that's all I'm saying. Which is of course because I could always totally count on you.

I loved Tommy Sanborne back on Oak Street in San Miguel – back when you were modelling at City College and we were living in that loft? I wanted to marry Tommy and have his babies, but then you explained the facts of life to me and I was *ginormously* disappointed.

I don't think I ever forgave you for explaining the facts of life to me, Mom. I'm dead serious.

Then I loved Mr Wilder, my third grade teacher. Then I loved Sue Granger, who wouldn't give me the time of day. I loved Bobby Anderson's mother, I loved Ken Kesey's *One Flew Over the Cuckoo's Nest*, and I loved pressing my face against sun-hot pavement. I loved other people's pets, sleeping in your bed, reruns of *Taxi*, overpriced haircuts, blond surfer boys, and fishing off the Pacifica pier with Tony Giamotti (this was before you decided to become a healing therapist and we had to move – *again*).

Presently I'm not in love with anybody whatsoever, with the possible exception of Nana.

How about you?

*

'What I'm trying to ask is did she say anything about *me*?'
Mr Sullivan was wearing a pressed white long-sleeve cotton
shirt and an electric-blue bow tie, which is a pretty killer
combination on an elderly man (especially if he happens
to be a physical sciences teacher). He was carrying a
bouquet of wildflowers wrapped up in pink ribbon and a
box of expensive-looking chocolates.

We were sitting in Nana's hospital room where Nana
was now dead asleep after a long and grueling afternoon
workout hallucinating on legally prescribed pharmaceuti-
cals. Just before Mr Sullivan arrived she woke for a few
minutes and asked for a glass of water. She was hoarse and
could barely talk.

She turned to me and said, 'How's the back yard, Teddy?'
blinking her slow eyes like a sun-struck lizard.

'It's okay, Nana,' I told her. 'Go back to sleep.'

And so now Mr Sullivan decided to give me the third
degree about this deeply meaningful exchange!

I told him as patiently as I could, 'Just because she didn't
ask about you, Mr Sullivan, doesn't mean you aren't on
her mind.'

'Sure,' he said. 'Yeah, sure. But did she say anything
about me? About my past, say. Or about my deceased wife,
Doris?'

I've decided that even though Mr Sullivan's full of
bullshit it's probably the sort of bullshit Nana needs right
now.

'She only said one thing about the past, Mr Sullivan.
Would you like to hear what that one thing was?'

Mr Sullivan sprung alert in the room like some sort of
radar. He was homing in on invisible missiles and space-
craft. As soon as the next alien projectile entered our
personal air-spaces, Mr Sullivan would conveniently
explode.

'What's that?' Mr Sullivan asked me. 'What did Emma
say about the past?'

I showed him to the chair near the window. I offered
him a glass of Nana's ice water from a green plastic pitcher.
Then, when he was settled, I tried to tell him one last time.

'She said to tell Mr Sullivan not to worry. She said to let Teddy take care of *everything*.'

On Monday I opened a joint-savings account in Nana's and my names where I deposited this healthy wad of cash I found buried in the back yard.

$33,456.37.

Nice chunk of change, huh? Then I forged (quite expertly, I might add) Nana's and Grandpa's signatures on the appropriate incoming pension and social-security checks. These added up to another cool five thousand, easy.

I bought myself a pair of Levis and six pairs of white tube-sox. Then I bought tea, bread, milk, canned soup, and new curtains for the picture window. Those old ones were getting rather tatty and hand-soiled.

Anyway – who needs paisley?

I also turned over a xerox of the following typewritten letter to Officer Rodrigues at the Police Station. I figured you might appreciate a copy? He's *your* father, after all.

Dear Emma

Let's face it. We've never gotten along. What more's left to say?

Mrs Stansfield is a big pain in the butt, but she's a decent cook and she's finished with menopause and she doesn't drive me crazy with a lot of false politeness all the time like some old bats I know. She's an annoying old cow and I just may love her.

Best of luck,
Marvin

P.S. Give my regards to the kids.

Now take a good look at Grandpa's signature, Mom. Notice the upright slope of the letters, and the backward-facing loop on the capital M? Those are the sure signposts of a really anti-type individual. Emotionally independent, proud, unappreciated, slightly vain. But hardly the living embodiment of Satan, so far as I can tell. I mean, there's actually no *law* against being emotionally inexpressive, is there?

If I were you, Mom, I'd sure hope not.

After I gave Officer Rodrigues this copy of the letter he had me give a formal statement and sign an affidavit. Then he swung himself around his small, cluttered cubicle for a while, slamming lots of drawers very self-importantly.

When I left, he shook my hand in a way Dad never did.

'You take good care of your Nana,' Officer Rodrigues said.

'Don't worry,' I told him. 'I will.'

Tonight, I'm sitting in Nana's 'office' listening to the Pet Shop Boys on my Sony Walkman and drinking a healthy (but not overly indulgent) dose of Nana's exorbitant brandy. I've replaced the fuse out back, cleared away the various rubbish items (empty potato chip bags mostly, Dixie cups and candy wrappers), and stacked Nana's multi-volume literary project very neatly on Nana's (formerly Grandpa's) antique rolltop deak. I've replaced a few stray pistols and rounds of ammunition in Grandpa's glass-cased cabinet in my room, bolted it up tight with the key, and mailed the key to Officer Rodrigues, care of his department.

Pretty efficient for a high-school drop-out and repeat juvenile offender – huh, Mom?

There's this big yellow cat I've let in from the back yard, and it's chewing on some sort of extinguished, moistly defeathering biped while purring with manifest contentment. You know why I like cats, Mom? Because they distribute their pleasure like light or energy. They don't keep it selfishly to themselves, like most people I know.

So while this yellow cat's busily chewing the plasma out of some fellow animal-creature I smoke a little reefer, imbibe a little brandy, and browse languidly among the weird, refracted dreams and revelations of Nana's lately inspired literary endeavors. I can't call it a 'diary', exactly, since its grasp of reality is rather ephemeral at best. (But then – whose grasp of reality isn't?) Nana's handwriting, however, is extremely legible, and she's got a pretty good imagination, especially for someone of her generation who hasn't had the benefit of modern hallucinogenics, Nintendo, death-rock or MTV.

In other words, Nana's diary definitely has its moments.

It's very weird, Mom, to read about the lives of people to whom I'm so unintimately related. And guess what I've stumbled upon? Vast interior consciousnesses, Mom. Slumbering undiscovered continents, vanished civilizations, sub-tropical dreams of sex and money and glory and love. Entire geographies of personality – and they exist in people who exist entirely independently from myself!

Imagine that.

If anybody in any of my infinitely monotonous high school classes had given me even the slightest indication that history is something that exists inside the hearts of people I know and not just in smelly old palaces and battlefields, well, maybe I wouldn't have cut so many classes. Maybe I wouldn't have forged so many official and unofficial letters to and from various administrative personnel. Maybe I wouldn't have tried diverting public funds to my own cozy little savings account at the good old Bank of America, and you wouldn't have felt obligated to get me out of town so *fast*. Maybe I would have *learned*, Mom. Just maybe.

But every time I went to history class what did they keep telling me? The fucking goddamn Missouri Compromise – Jesus fucking Christ. And here I've got this Nana I've never met before with more good history inside her than fifty textbooks. Maybe even fifty-one textbooks, Mom. Who knows?

So what have I learned in my week of rummaging about in Nana's memories? Well, I'll tell you.

Hate is a terrible thing to live with. And forgiveness is the only way of living with it that I know.

Forgiveness, Mom. We should learn to exercise it, like muscles or vocabulary. And we shouldn't forgive other people out of some weird selfless altruism. We should forgive in order to live with ourselves. It's fundamentally a pretty selfish exercise, and one I'm doing my best to learn.

So that's why I forgive you, Mom. I am sitting here in the midst of Nana's most cluttery and intimate room, surrounded by all the hastily scribbled anger Nana could never adequately express, and I forgive you. I forgive you the same way you should forgive Nana, and the same way Nana should forgive Grandpa.

So listen up.

- I forgive you, Mom, for your succession of flaky boyfriends, none of whom was flakier or more unforgivable than my irreversibly genetic progenitor, Dad.
- I forgive you for your lousy home-making capabilities, not to mention your lousy cooking.
- I forgive you for your conducting Astral Projection Seminars in our apartment in Costa Mesa, where you insisted on using me as your demonstration dummy even though I was only six years old at the time. And I forgive you for yelling at me afterwards for being so lousy at Astral Projection that I made you look bad in front of your friends (how many times do I have to tell you, Mom? I'm just *not* a very spiritual being).
- I forgive you for taking so long to bail me out of juvie that first time I got arrested for forgery. Even though I nearly got raped by some guy. Even though you acted like the crime I committed had been against you personally and not against the stupid Bank of America or the Fullerton High School Credit system (neither of whom would have missed that lousy few thousand bucks, believe me).
- I forgive you your, like, totally awful taste in men (this one's worth forgiving you for twice).
- I forgive you for never once admitting you were wrong.
- I forgive you for not teaching me how to forgive.
- I forgive you for my anger. Which was once your

anger. Which was once Nana's, and Grandpa's, ad infinitum, amen.

See how easy that was?

Try it, Mom. Try saying it just this once. Miles away you are and inaccessible except by fax. Yet you can say it. With your own two lips you can make it real. Not just words, Mom. Bodies, lives, substrata, rocks. Roiling memories and vast, implicate communities of ghosts. Our own flesh and stomach, Mom. Make them real. Then maybe you can start feeling a little more real yourself.

Say it, Mom. I believe in you. And I know you believe in me, too.

I forgive you, Mom.

So to sum up: there's just me, this yellow cat (purringly asleep now, and mortally dispossessed of its bald well-masticated sparrow – being as I've just tossed it out the window), this nice warm room, and Nana's memories and brandy circulating in my body like a faint soporific.

Deep breath, exhale. And then another slow, deep breath.

(Words aren't just something you speak, Mom. Words are something you breathe as well.)

Em-ma. Em-ma.

My nana and your mom, Mom. The doctors tell me she'll be home soon.

Wouldn't it be nice if we could both be here to meet her? In this awful suburban ranch-style house where you refuse to admit you were ever born?

I guess I've always felt cellularly lapsed and colorless, Mom. Compared to you and your wildly imagined life, that is.

So sometimes I say these like prayers, see? Prayers but without a god to address them to. Prayers to myself and the people I know – but until now I never had the courage to share them with anybody else out loud before. What I used to do was say these prayers to myself, and then get

194

mad at you because you didn't hear me. Isn't that a stupid waste of energy?

So this time I'll speak it. For you and me, Mom. For you, me, Nana, Grandpa, Uncle Thomas (who I still haven't met), and whatever cousins are out there, and that wide glistening web-work of kinship and demesne you keep pretending doesn't contain us anymore, doesn't describe and invest the genetic stuff of Who We Are. I'll speak it like one of your mantras. I'll speak it with all the spiritual integrity you pretend I possess even though I'm nothing more than this rather ragged, sexually dysfunctional, mildly unassuming adolescent with a criminal record and almost no concrete professional ambitions.

I'll speak it now, Mom. Are you listening?

Come to California, Mom, where you've always belonged. Run a damp rag across your old garage-encysted dune-buggy, saddle it up and drive back down the only roads you know. California, the home of the next great super-race, bathed in cosmic vibrations, bristling with earth-quakes and mighty spiritual thunder. We grow bigger brains out here, Mom. Smoother and rounder buttocks, blonder hair, sandier beaches, better sex, cooler wine coolers, longer woodier piers, flatter stomachs and bluer, more lustrous eyes than all the rest of the world put together.

Already I'm one of them, Mom. Californians – they visit me in my dreams.

Beautiful sun-bathed Californians wearing tank-top T-shirts, Spandex bicycle pants and yellow terry-cloth head-bands. Men and women who stand poised on the brink of their own metaphysical destinies, stunning seismic tem-blors stroking the ground beneath their toes. They massage my skin with sun-screens and conditioners, Vitamin E lotion and body-musk. Out here, Mom, we've given up altogether on stress reduction. Out here we're talking about something called 'stress-management'.

Come to California for Christmas, Mom, where the beaches remain sunny all year long. Come to California and start being all those impossible people you've never been before. We'll show Nana, right? We'll teach Nana games she could play inside her own heart she never dreamed of. Because when you get right down to it, Mom, you want to know what's *really* wrong with America?

America isn't California.

And thank Heavens.

Love,
Teddy

P.S. I've got to run along now before that sweet young thing at Speedy-Quick closes his fax for the night. I've saved all Nana's diaries which I plan to sink into a time-vault, kind of like the Warren Commission Report, to be released only fifty years after Nana's parlous demise. (If you're good, though, I might tell you about them someday.)

And considering these diaries are being reserved for posterity, I've gone ahead and made just the *teeniest* stylistic emendations here and there, adjustments for rhythm, clarity, dramatic effect, you know. Being a semi-professional forger, I can slip in and out of white sheets like these undetected, sort of like a disembodied burglar. (It's amazing, by the way, how much reality you can compose and discompose with a cheap ball-point pen. Even when that reality belongs to somebody else entirely.)

I've hardly made any changes of any real significance, however.

P.P.S. While we're at it, I've taken the additional liberty of hiring building contractors to pave over the back yard with this like super-duper pebbly gray concrete. I think Nana's gardening days are over – don't you?